KT-381-550

BENDER'S BOOT

Bloody Kansas, 1872, and Conroy McClure is searching for his missing brother. At a remote inn, he becomes involved with an evil family and, in particular, the she-devil of a daughter who ensnares men in a murderous web of sensuality. Local vigilantes storm the inn, intent on lynching the entire family. But the killers have fled, taking McClure with them. Buried in the adjacent orchard are twelve brutally mutilated bodies, including a little girl who was clearly buried alive. But what is the fate of Conroy McClure?

MARK BANNERMAN

BENDER'S BOOT

Complete and Unabridged

LINFORD
Leicester

First published in Great Britain in 2004 by
Robert Hale Limited
London

First Linford Edition
published 2006
by arrangement with
Robert Hale Limited
London

British Library CIP Data

Bannerman, Mark
    Bender's boot.—Large print ed.—
    Linford western library
    1. Western stories
    2. Large type books
    I. Title
    823.9'14 [F]

    ISBN 1–84617–126–1

Published by
F. A. Thorpe (Publishing)
Anstey, Leicestershire

Set by Words & Graphics Ltd.
Anstey, Leicestershire
Printed and bound in Great Britain by
T. J. International Ltd., Padstow, Cornwall

*To my good friends Keith Hayward
and Karin Robinshaw.
With thanks for their invaluable
technical advice.*

1

Conroy McClure eased his salt encrusted eyelids open, then shut them, not liking the knife-like sting that blurred his vision. Wincingly, he tried again.

He wondered if he was in the next world. One thing was certain: it wasn't Heaven, so it must be the other place. Or maybe it was a sort of waiting-room, where you were put while your life was checked out, and all your sins totted up, along with any good deeds you might have done — and then whichever was the greater would tip the balance, sending you to Paradise or Hell.

Right now, Conroy McClure couldn't recall a single good thing he had ever achieved in his life. In fact, he couldn't recall anything.

He felt as if his head were enclosed in a tight metal band. Every time he attempted movement, pain lanced through him. His clothing was sodden. His mouth was coated with salt, and he was sure his innards were overflowing with sea water. When he inhaled, he gurgled and wheezed and was on the verge of throwing up. He'd probably done his share of that already. The light was grey, even so, glancing aloft, he realized that he was in a cave. From its roof, shadowy stalactites reached down like accusing fingers. He was sprawled on his back, nodules of rock punishing his spine.

He reached a conclusion: his pain was so sharp he must still be alive — but only just.

That noise? Was it voices involved in angry discussion about his fate? No, it was the sea pounding against a shore, and the howl of a storm. He shivered, suffered a spasm that intensified his torment.

He groaned.

He felt a gentle touch on his face and heard the soft, soothing murmuring of words entwined with the racket of wind and sea. A girl was leaning over him, her hair brushing his cheek, her face seeming strangely luminous in the gloom. He wondered if she was some sort of angel.

'Who are you?' he croaked.

'Maria Schoenfelt,' she responded. Her inflection was German — and, despite his lack of memory, hauntingly familiar.

He forced his lips to move again. 'My name is . . . I am . . . ' He somehow choked on his words. It felt as if tentacles of some frantic octopus were reaching along the corridors of his mind, probing like jelly into the deepest corners, searching, searching — but finding nothing.

'Can't remember my name,' he admitted.

She emitted what could have been a sigh of relief. 'Then you will need help.'

Exasperation flared in him. 'What's happened to me?'

'You were washed up by the sea,

more dead than alive. I believe a ship went down, out there in the bay. I have not seen any other survivors. I was walking along the shore. It was lucky I found you. I dragged you up to this cave. You will live now, I think.'

'But why were you on the shore?'

Again she sighed, this time a deep, shuddering sigh. 'I ran away from my father. He abused me. I have many bruises. He . . . ' Her voice trailed off, smothered by the roar of the outside waves.

'Where is this place?' he asked.

'Texas.'

'Texas! How . . . ?'

'Come daylight,' she interrupted, 'we will go into town. You must see a doctor. You have been badly hurt.'

'Yes,' he gasped. 'I don't know why I'm still alive.'

'It is your head. A terrible injury. It is like a cracked eggshell!'

'Oh, God!' He rested back on the hard rock of the cave floor. 'It has destroyed my memory.'

'You must sleep now,' she whispered. 'I will watch over you.'

'Maria, I am truly beholden to you, so grateful.' He closed his eyes, submitted to the pain in his head. Presently he drifted into relieving blackness.

★ ★ ★

As the grey fingers of dawn probed the sky, she awakened him. The storm had abated, the sea quieted. Presently, she helped him to his feet, encouraged him to work the stiffness from his limbs.

'You have slept for a whole day and night,' she said.

Every part of his body felt bruised, but the pain in his head was the worst. He wondered if his brains were spilling out. He reached up, probed his skull with tentative fingers. He could feel crusted blood, even the indentation, but the bone appeared not to be splintered. His head had taken an almighty knock, shaking it beyond belief, but it had not

5

burst open. He swayed with dizziness.

'You have a very thick skull,' she said.

His nod made him wince.

He gazed at her face closely for the first time. Shock ran through him and he didn't know why. It was as if her face was familiar, but he could not recall from where. She was a pretty girl, maybe in her early twenties.

Later, they walked along a wild shoreline, the smell of washed-up kelp in their nostrils. They passed through tall wind-sculpted dunes, anchored by wild sea oats. Various fragments of wreckage had been washed up on to the sands. They encountered a giant turtle, resting, but it moved into the water at their approach. Meanwhile, the sun was rising, flooding balmy warmth into the day, turning the sea into deep azure and causing heatwaves to shimmer and dance before them. Gulls screeched at them indignantly, as if gossiping about the storm, and presently whooping cranes flew overhead. He moved slowly, relying on her arm, sometimes feeling the comforting nudge of her breast against him. There was a wiry strength to her.

Conroy was a stocky, short man with thick black eyebrows and dark hair, now tangled, which hung to his shoulders. His complexion was the colour of suntanned sandalwood. His features were even and handsome, adorned by a horseshoe moustache.

Eventually, they encountered a dozen small clinker-built fishing boats, drawn up on the sands, then they took a path inland, moving through groves of palm trees interspersed with high grasses. They met no other persons until they reached the outskirts of a small town. Here they saw a weathered finger-board, its faded lettering proclaiming: WELCOME TO VALPARADO — Population 957. In an untidy and somewhat sad scrawl, somebody had altered it to 956.

They walked through an orchard of ruby-red grapefruits and eventually reached a centre of habitation, which consisted of terraces of low white houses, constructed of adobe and stone and grouped around a central plaza, currently about half an acre of freshly drying mud; on one side this was shaded by a line of giant oaks, beneath which a number of mules were hitched to a rail. Some branches had fallen in the high winds. On the opposite side of the plaza was an old church, its corners supported by heavy earthen buttresses, its façade decorated long ago by Spanish craftsmen, and alongside was the *cabildo* with its clock tower. The inhabitants were stirring from their homes, taking down barricades that had been erected as protection from the storm, and putting up stalls in the plaza. Many of them wore straw sombreros. People paid little attention to the man and girl, their conversation mostly centred around the violence of the recent weather. Now, with the sun brassy in the cloudless sky, the heat was increasing, and everything moved at a leisurely pace, even the goats, and dogs that could not be bothered to bark. Conroy noticed the strong Mexican influence in all he saw, but gradually he became aware of many German names as well. Several stores bore German signs.

'I have some money,' Maria told him. 'I will find us lodgings.'

'Why are you being so downright good to me?' he asked.

'Because, you are as much in need of help as I am.'

'What can I do to help you?' he enquired, but she did not answer.

Maria approached an old man who sat in a rocking chair smoking his pipe in the shade of the oak trees. She asked if lodgings might be found.

'*Sí, señorita*,' he responded, his smile revealing gold teeth. His face was liver-spotted. He pointed with the stem of his pipe to where a narrow street led off the plaza. 'Next to the fandango hall.'

They found the guesthouse with its porch supported by heavy timbers, and they entered. There, seeing nobody in attendance, Maria pressed the bell upon the counter. A prune-faced woman shuffled out from the back, smoothing her skirt into place.

'We wish to book a room,' Maria said. She hesitated, then added, 'We are husband and wife, and have fallen on . . . unfortunate circumstances.'

The woman looked doubtful, but when she saw that the girl had produced gold coins, her attitude changed.

Hearing Maria refer to him as her husband, Conroy felt no resentment. Her closeness was something he did not want to lose. He admired her confident manner.

The woman showed them to a small adobe at the rear of the house, and left them.

'Maria, will your father come looking for you?' he asked.

She frowned. 'I pray not.'

He looked at her, expecting her to continue, but she did not. She spread the blankets on the double bed.

'You should rest now,' she said. 'You must take off your wet clothes. I will hang them out to dry in the sun.'

He hesitated and she laughed. 'Remember, we are Mr and Mrs Schoenfelt.'

He stripped off, covered himself with a blanket.

'I think,' he said, 'that you are an angel and I am lucky.'

She cocked her head in her easy manner and smiled. '*Ja*, I am an angel, your special angel.'

But she did not say he was lucky.

2

Later, she took him along quaint streets to a freshly plastered adobe house between the funeral parlour and the barber's. Its weather-worn shingle announced: *Doctor Joshua Miller, expert in treating Syphilis, Diabetes, Urinary Problems and Female Diseases.*

Doctor Miller was a rotund, heavily moustached man with protruding eye ridges and a grave demeanour. He examined Conroy's head wound as if it was the most serious injury he'd ever encountered. Then, for a long moment, he peered into the patient's eyes, expressing satisfaction that the pupils were not enlarged.

'How did this happen?' he asked. 'It looks like somebody hit you with a hammer.'

Conroy tried to express his puzzlement with a shake of his head, but he gave up because it hurt too much. 'I can't remember,' he said.

'I believe he survived a shipwreck,' Maria explained.

The doctor nodded. 'I know a ship went down in the storm. You are the only survivor I've heard about.'

He washed Conroy's wound, padded it dry, then with some scissors cut away small pieces of torn skin. Afterwards, he applied ointment and wound a bandage around Conroy's head like a turban.

'You will live,' Doctor Miller explained, 'but you will always have a dent. Maybe your memory will come back, maybe not. If it does not, you won't be worried about the past. That might not be a bad thing.'

Conroy wasn't so sure. He swallowed hard. Life without a past was unnerving. He was dependent on Maria; thank God he had her. Even so, it was not good to be so reliant.

The doctor supplied him with some catnip tea, to be taken thrice daily.

Conroy shook his hand and thanked him.

Maria drew out a purse and paid the medical man in gold coins, after which they returned to the adobe behind the guesthouse.

Having ensured his comfort, she left him, saying there were things she needed to do, things to buy. He lay on the bed, still feeling weak. He wished he had money to give her, but he knew his pockets were empty. Presently, lulled by the hum of bees outside his window, he slept.

An hour later she was back, looking pleased with herself. She had brought tortillas, fresh cheese, bread, some peaches and a bottle of wine. It was frugal fare, but soon they were eating with relish.

'I have got a job, working in a hardware store,' she said, her mouth full like a happy child. 'I will earn enough money to keep us in this place until we find somewhere else.'

He gazed at her, noticing how she

took the word 'we' for granted.

Her sweetly expressive prettiness was of a type that many fortunate girls possessed — the type he had encountered before, but could not remember where. Another girl, another place . . . or the same girl?

She showed no shyness before him. She bathed at the pump at the back of their adobe, her hair gathered in a swirl, her cherry-pink nipples and ivory-pale breasts bared and glistening in the sunlight. As she rubbed soap under her arms and down over her ribs, his glance lingered on her lissom body, and she laughed and he knew she enjoyed feeling the warmth of his eyes. He wondered why she trusted him so profoundly. Yes, he thought, it is as if she has known me before . . .

For a week, she left him in the mornings to go to work. He rested, feeling his strength flowing back. He fought a battle with his brain, trying to cudgel it into recollections of his past — but there was only blankness. He could do nothing but swim with the tide.

At night they lay in each other's arms, and she stirred a passion in him that needed little encouragement. They answered a desperate need in each other.

'You have not forgotten how to make a woman feel good,' she whispered. 'We must get married and make it real.'

'How can you marry somebody who does not know himself?' he sighed. 'Maybe I am already married.'

'We must take a chance on that,' she said. 'Nobody will treat it as a crime if you cannot remember. As time goes on, it will become even easier for you. You will build up new memories.'

At night, when they lay sated in each other's embrace, he drew from her the story of her past.

'My mother died a year ago,' she confided. 'She was a sick woman. My father bullied her into death. I . . . ' For a moment she was overcome with grief, and she wept in his arms until she could go on. 'Afterwards, he turned his bullying on me. He whipped me and did unspeakable things. He humiliated me in front of his friends, treated me like a slave. I couldn't stand it any longer. So I ran away. For three days and three nights I walked, all the time scared that he would follow me. I reached the coast. That was when that terrible storm blew up, coming in from the Gulf. I've never seen anything like it. I do not know why, but I found myself running along the beach, wading in the waves. I didn't much care whether the sea sucked me in or not. I stumbled over something in the darkness. I thought it was flotsam washed up, but then I realized it was a body — and you were still alive!'

He loved the guttural yet soft murmur of her voice and the way she told the story. He tried to get her to tell him more of her childhood, but she would not, preferring to whisper intimate words about their love.

He understood how innocent a child

felt, because there were no past sins or guilt to drag at him. But he sensed it couldn't last. Sin anchored you, tied you to yourself. A life without sin propelled a man towards ethereal happiness that, in truth, could not exist this side of Heaven.

★ ★ ★

As his strength returned, his headache became less severe, and he took short walks through the town, seeking anything or anybody that might be familiar, but he encountered only people who clearly knew him no better than he knew them. He found them friendly and easygoing, and he asked as many questions as he could without appearing overinquisitive. Sometimes he would squat on the ground with them and share beans and chilli, using a tortilla for a spoon, his ears soaking up all they said. Even so, he learned little that could link him to his past, and the blank space in his mind became inhabited by a sensation of fear, of foreboding.

The following week, Maria explained that the proprietor of the store where she worked required a manager to run the place. She had suggested Conroy, and the proprietor said he sounded *El Bueno* — a good man. Conroy gladly took up the offer, though he was unfamiliar with such employment. However, he took to it well. Both he and Maria exchanged pleasantries with the customers and strove to please them. Within a few days, so expert did Conroy become at salesmanship, that the proprietor withdrew to concentrate on importing stock from the north on his string of burros, and Conroy and Maria ran the business.

The store was a long, low building, its roof supported by massive hand-hewn beams. Above its doorway hung a sign saying *Tienda Barata*, which meant 'cheap store'. The place was a warren of wagon and carriage furniture, kegs of nails, soldered kitchenware, coal oil lanterns, horse tack, knives, tools, razors, shaving mugs, saws, planes and augers, and even some religious paintings of Christ crucified, the Virgin Mary and many of the Saints. In addition, there was a lively trade in chewing tobacco, wooden *santitos*, playing cards and toothbrushes. Conroy and Maria spread their stocks wide for all to see.

Plump Mexican *señoras* and German *fraus*, in lace shawls and voluminous skirts, frequented the store, finding the stock fairly priced with credit readily available. They paid in several different coinages. Generally his customers appeared to put beauty before use, preferring to adorn life and celebrate it.

Children came in swarms to see the display, but they did not touch the items. They were precocious, but polite and avidly inquisitive. Sometimes Conroy would reward them with cones of brown sugar.

He learned that Germans had been

among the first European immigrants to come to Texas during its decade as a republic. Texas had been recognized as a sovereign state and adopted a liberal policy towards foreign immigration. This was so much so, that in 1843, the legislature had ordered the publication of the laws of Texas in German. When the state became part of the United States, this made little difference to the cosmopolitan population. Europeans built ranches and grazed their longhorn cattle on the lush prairies to the north.

Three months after they had taken on the store, Conroy and Maria were married in the local church — a quiet ceremony spoken in Spanish, attended by no guests, for they were generally understood to be husband and wife already. There was no celebration. They took their vows, gazing into each other's eyes and smiling happily in the knowledge that the union between them was bonded. As he did not know his real name, he took hers, strange as it was — Schoenfelt. Soon after, they rented a modest adobe house on the outskirts of the town. It was run down and he replastered its old walls, inside and out. He cleared the lush crop of weeds from its roof, and repaired several holes. At the back, he built a small windmill, which he used to pump water. Close by, he planted a vegetable patch of corn and beans.

Maria fed him well, with thick soups, *gefilte* fish, stewed chicken, *knische* potatoes, and wonderful sweet cakes. Sometimes they played checkers. On most evenings, they sat on rawhide chairs beneath an awning made of mesquite, and gazed up at pinpoints of light in the universe. As they talked, he tried to fit together the shadowy familiarities that flitted through his head, but they were too vague, too obscure to make sense.

And on Sundays they attended mass at the church where they had wed.

All might have been well, but he felt restless and that he was living in a vacuum. It was as though he were in some sort of balloon, weighted down by the large pebble that was his past — a pebble he could not reach or even catch sight of. At times he would growl with frustration.

Conroy's love for Maria deepened. Sometimes, he could hardly believe that she was real. She told him little of her past, nothing of the father who had abused her. But she delighted him with her happy disposition, and only occasionally did he catch her off guard, with the brightness gone from her face and replaced by some inner rage. Her father, he thought; she must be thinking of how her father treated her. This, in turn, made him angry. How could anybody maltreat this girl, who hadn't an ounce of wickedness in her? So he reasoned.

On some afternoons, when the store was closed, Conroy would join the local fishermen in their skiffs and row out to sea. He was still inwardly afraid of the water, and he felt this might overcome his fear. He would help with the nets, hauling in the catches of tuna and other fish he did not recognize. On several occasions he saw dorsal fins cleaving the surface, and his companions would laugh nervously and say 'Maneaters', because they knew these belonged to the great predators of the ocean — white sharks. Once, one came close, powering through the water sideways and beating its tail. For a moment it swam alongside their craft, its awesome serrated teeth bared, as if trying to warn off its competitors for food.

On another day, when they encountered sharks, one of the fishermen winked at Conroy and said, 'Watch!'

The man lifted up a gaff, held it poised like a lance, and gazed overboard into the water. Shortly, his arm jerked downwards and he lifted the gaff to display a small shark, snapping and squirming, no more than three feet long. He slashed open the shark's belly with his knife, unleashing a stream of bloody innards. He immediately threw the creature back into the sea. There came a sudden explosion of water, whipped by threshing tails. Fins criss-crossed the surface as sharks snapped at the disembowelled fish. Spray plumed up, catching the men watching from the boat.

As the commotion subsided, Conroy looked at his shirt front. It was splattered with blood.

* * *

One morning as he stood behind his store counter, he looked at an old copy of the *Galveston Gazette*, and on an inside page a report caught his eye. It told of a terrible family by the name of Bender, who had murdered countless people in Kansas, and how they had fled when the vigilantes attempted to arrest them. The family had consisted of the mother and father, and son and daughter. The latter was said to be very pretty. A Mexican sea captain called Don Pieppo claimed that the family had drowned when his ship had sunk in a hurricane off the Gulf Coast, near to the town of Valparado.

That evening, Conroy showed Maria the article. She was leaning over a bowl, sponging black dye into her hair.

'Do you think this has something to do with me?' he asked. 'Maybe it's where I came from. Maybe I'm one of the Benders!'

She wrapped her hair in a towel and scanned the article. 'Too fanciful to be true,' she said.

Why was it too fanciful to be true? For some reason, he was too fearful to ask her.

'How come you're dying your hair, Maria? It sure makes you look different.'

She shrugged her shoulders. 'It makes me look better,' she said.

The story of the shipwreck and of the Bender family lingered in his mind, haunting him like a jigsaw piece for which he could find no place yet knew it belonged.

He started to have dreams, visions of

suffocating greenness that grew darker and darker, with slimy, savage creatures rising from below, shredding his flesh; and, from his mouth, incandescent bubbles flowing upwards, gradually becoming fewer until there were no more. And he could not breathe and was fighting, struggling, but it seemed nothing could arrest his descent. Only then would he awake, crying out, covered in chilling sweat, sucking air into heaving lungs. Slowly, he would become aware of Maria's soothing voice, her gentle touch, drawing him back to the temporary sanctuary of the present, drawing him into the comforting warmth of her body.

3

It was two and a half years earlier.

'I will kill the sow this afternoon,' Jason Bender told his father. It was a task he'd been looking forward to.

Jason Bender, twenty-two years old, was six feet tall and as strong as a bull, and he enjoyed macho posturing. He might have been handsome had his eyes not been so close-set and his teeth yellow and crooked. His habit of chewing tobacco and indiscriminately spitting it out in brown streams tended to repulse some people.

'She is past mating,' he went on. 'The meat will be stringy, but it will be good enough for the guests.'

The father, Old John, grunted his agreement. He seldom said much, professing ignorance of the language, but he understood more than he let on, particularly curse-words. He and his wide-hipped, tallow-faced wife Almira had emigrated from Germany, where he'd earned his living as a carpenter and balloon seamster. In fact, he'd once flown across Germany by means of a home-made balloon.

Jason went into the kitchen section of the cabin, and picked up the big butcher's knife. It was ideal for cutting throats. It had done so many times. Blood turned foul was clotted darkly on the shaft, and the blade, once displaying a proud 'Made in Sheffield', had assumed a dull slough that had never been washed clean. The only maintenance it received was the honing of the cutting edge.

Jason's sister, two years his junior, stood watching him. Just having her eyes on him caused a tingling sensation. He'd tried to convince himself that she wasn't really his sister, and she'd been put on this earth for his pleasure, but that didn't somehow wash, so he'd given up moralizing and just enjoyed her body whenever he could. Sometimes, however, she had other ideas, and this irked him.

She had a round face and broad mouth. Her eyes were a striking green, her hair possessing the glint of copper. It was incredible that she was such a good-looking female, because she had apparently been bred by parents as ugly as sin. Here, in Labette County, south-east Kansas, their cabin was nine miles from Cherryvale. It lay on a slight prairie elevation, a hundred yards back from the trail that ran from Fort Scott and the Old Osage Mission to Independence. To the north was a mound of rocks that was thickly peppered with sandstone. The cabin commanded a good view, both east and west, along the trail. This was bleak December and, with the buckbush and ground cloaked in snow, the land had the appearance of absolute desolation. Such gangs as the Daltons and the James had escaped the clutches of law-enforcement officers in this godforsaken terrain more than once.

The cabin served as an inn and

general store, and had the word GROCERIES painted on a board above its front door. The entire frame-built place was no more than sixteen by twenty-four feet. Its interior was crude. No lathes, plastering or decoration adorned the walls. There was only one room, but the rear third was partitioned off by a calico curtain. The front section contained a counter, and shelves lined the walls. Upon these was a meagre selection of flour, eggs, sugar, hammers and nails, which were sold to passers-by. Behind the counter were a heavily stained walnut table and two benches, one of which backed up against the curtain.

The front section also had several mattresses and a rocking chair for the comfort of family and overnight guests.

Gripping the knife, Jason stepped out into the raw wind, bullish shoulders hunched against the cold. He hurried through the assorted outbuildings towards the hog-pen, his feet leaving large prints in the snow.

He went round the main barn, which was somewhat larger than the other outbuildings, and entered the shed that stood next to the hog-pen. He removed his coat and rolled the shirtsleeves back from his strong arms. He put on a worn and bloodstained apron.

Fastened to the roof of the shed were several hooks for hanging up carcasses while he eviscerated them. He would keep the sow's heart and liver for family use. The guts and intestines he would feed to the remaining hogs. They would welcome this, because the family never went to the expense of giving them corn, just letting them dig for grass and roots. The rest of the carcass would provide joints and chops that could be salted away and used when required for the guests who came to the inn.

He prepared his sticker and boner, honing them to sharpness on an oilstone block, finishing them off with slow purposeful strokes along his butcher's steel.

He was conscious of ferment pulsing

through his veins. It was the same sensation he experienced when he was about to mount a female, particularly his sister, ignoring her objections to his clumsiness in the blind torrent of his passion.

Slotting the knives in his belt, he gathered up a coil of thick rope and stepped from the shed and went through the gate into the hog-pen.

The other hogs shifted away uneasily, but the lazy sow, a razor-back, allowed him to approach her without complaining. He fastened his rope through her nose ring, kicked her to her feet and half dragged her to the adjacent shed. Only when he had fastened her right foreleg to a back leg, and she was completely immobilized, did she realize that something unpleasant was afoot, but by then it was too late. She was threshing hopelessly as he drew the big knife. He plunged it deep into the beast's throat, slashing it towards the aorta, delighting in the way the blood fountained up. The sow's gurgling shrieks were deafening, drowning out the howl of the outside wind, but within ten minutes she had made her last kick and her wretched existence was over.

Sweating with the effort, glistening with blood, Jason lifted the carcass to a hook, using his primitive hoist.

Over the next hour he cut, sliced and chopped with ruthless efficiency, for he was well experienced in butchery. Standing in a pool of gore, his mind drifted back to his last visit to Cherryvale.

In town, he had heard talk. Everybody was worked up about how certain folks had disappeared in the territory, and how Labette County was said to be the place to search for missing kin. Apparently, the last communication received from several of the vanished folk, as they headed west, had come from the Osage Mission. In addition, the township trustee of Cherryvale had received no less than six letters from concerned relatives. The community was downright uneasy about the situation, and men went about armed and kept their womenfolk locked up at home when alone. Concern was illustrated by the increase in church attendances. Folks just felt safer being together. Meanwhile, there was talk of a vigilante group being formed to investigate matters.

Jason and his father had listened uneasily.

★   ★   ★

Yes, Katie Bender was a good-looking young woman, slim and willowy. She was an easy talker with a down-to-earth manner, and at times she would hoot with laughter, mostly at the misfortunes of others. Her hair was long and sleek. Her skin, despite its frequent exposure to hostile elements, was the colour of ivory. When she went to town, it seemed there wasn't a male person, young or old, who was unaware of her presence. She walked along with her skirt hiked up out of the dust, not caring that other womenfolk strove to turn their men's heads in alternative directions in the belief that she was a brazen hussy.

At home, she was not averse to cursing at her lumbering father, and he generally took it and scurried away to do what he was told. Even so, contempt blazed from her eyes every time she looked at him. As for her brother Jason, she tolerated his roughness, sometimes being afraid of his fierce manner.

Both Katie and her mother professed to possess clairvoyant powers, and claimed that they could communicate with the next world. They worked with candles and chalk and said they could cure the sick, but they never seemed sufficiently concerned about the welfare of others to put these powers into use.

Now, Katie happened to glance from the window of the cabin, and immediately her heartbeat quickened. She turned to her father, who was warming his feet by the stove.

'Go and tell Jason there is a rider coming in,' she said.

4

Old Man Bender rose and said, '*Ja*. It is good.' He pulled on his boots and went outside. He was sixty years old, heavily built, with a rat's-nest beard and a body covered in hair. His barrel chest and long arms gave him the appearance of a grizzly bear, and his crouching, cloddish gait enhanced that impression.

The light was fading, the curtain of snow thickening. He made his way down to the shed adjoining the hog-pen.

'Jason, there is a rider coming up the trail. We have a customer.'

Jason was finishing his butchery of the sow, catching a plentiful supply of blood in a bucket for future sausage-making. He did not immediately respond to his father's announcement, just grunted to himself, but he turned away from the sow's carcass, removed his bloody apron and shook it. He found a piece of rag and wiped his arms down.

'A customer — *ja!*' he grunted, and a trembling in his hands betrayed excitement.

The entire Bender family was in the cabin's open doorway, braving the cold in their efforts to appear welcoming. The trail-weary stranger reined in his sorrel and half fell from the saddle. He was a shortish man, with the flaps of his muskrat cap pulled down about his ears. His movements were made awkward by his heavy buffalo coat. Jason's eyes dwelt on his footwear. Black, 'French calf', with a mass of fancy stitching on each boot-top. These were not a poor man's boots.

In the frigid air, the stranger's breath mingled with the steam from the horse's flanks. He shivered and said, 'Could sure do with some warm hospitality, something to eat and a night's lodging.'

'You come to the right place, mister,'

Katie Bender responded, her voice edged with Teutonic allurement. She turned to her brother. 'Take care of his horse.'

Jason complied. He resented her bossing him around, but provided he got his rewards, he was resigned to suffering it. Anyway, now was not the time for arguments.

The visitor raised his head, caught the girl's eye and clearly liked what he saw. A minute later he was inside the front section of the cabin, enjoying the warmth from the stove. Wordlessly, Old John took the buffalo coat and muskrat cap, shook the snow out of them and hung them on a hook behind the door. His wife stepped beyond the curtain, and the clink of cooking pans sounded.

Katie batted her eyes and gave the impression of being taken with the stranger, her smile following him. Her features were softened in the light of the single tallow candle set in a glass pie-dish; she might have been mistaken for an angel.

'It is so good to get somebody calling,' she murmured, keeping her voice low, in an intimate way. 'We do not get many visitors at this time of year.'

He nodded. 'It's a real pleasure to find a place so homely.'

'You sit down.' She nodded towards the bench on the far side of the walnut table. '*Ja*, with your back against the curtain. That is our place of honour. Motti will soon have some food ready. I will sit next to you. That is, if you don't object.'

He laughed. 'You surely may. Just being with you warms me up no end.'

The fact was, attractive females were rare in these parts, and to have one so attentive was quite something.

'You are not from around here, then?' she enquired, sliding close to him on the bench.

'Nope. Just passing through on my way home. Done some business in Cherryvale.'

'Oh, how interesting,' she said.

Old John was standing motionless in the corner of the room, practically invisible in the shadows. Outside, the wind rattled against the roof. It was developing into a real howler out there.

'What is your business, Mr . . . ?' Katie asked.

'Horse-trading,' came the reply. 'I just sold some good stock.'

'So it is a profitable business, eh?'

'Sure is.'

Katie eased her body against the stranger's, resting her hand on his, well aware that her firm, protrusive breasts were touching his arm.

He cleared his throat, looking as pleased as a bear with a honeypot.

'Sure will be good to sleep in a warm bed tonight,' he commented.

'I have heard tell,' she said, 'that the bed of a lonely man is never warm. Perhaps it does not have to be that way. It gets lonely for a girl out here, too.'

'Is that so?' he murmured, a huskiness in his voice.

She turned her head.

'Pappi,' she called, 'why not help Motti with supper? It is not fair to leave all the chores to her.'

Old John growled something and disappeared behind the curtain. Once concealed, he quietly opened a cupboard and lifted out a big hammer. The butcher's knife had been placed alongside it, still shiny with the sow's blood. The knife would come in handy shortly. He crept forward, exchanging a meaningful glance with his wife, Almira. He positioned himself behind the curtain, close to where the stranger's back bulged through the calico. The old man made sure his brawny, hirsute arms had ample room to swing the hammer.

Katie had debated whether a frolic with her companion might be pleasant before further business was conducted. Anything would be better than Jason's bullish coupling. But it was her time of the month and she was currently a little tired, although nobody would have suspected that from the immodest way she was acting. She consoled herself with the thought that there would be further opportunities soon enough.

Suddenly all the sweetness vanished from her face. 'Do it now!' she screamed.

Old John swung the hammer downward with the force of a poleaxe, finding his spot perfectly, the blow unimpeded by the thin calico.

As the guest dropped to the floor, half his skull cloven in, Katie sprang away, anxious not to be soiled by the splattering blood. There was more to follow as her father rushed around the curtain, the great butcher's knife in his hand. He stooped down, plunged the blade into the side of the man's neck and slashed it sideways, nigh severing the head.

Katie and her mother dragged the table away from the trapdoor in the floor with rehearsed precision. They grabbed the leather boot-strap that served as a handle and pulled it open. Fashioned from two-by-fours, a ladder led down some seven feet. Eighteen months ago, her father had obtained a well auger and bored this cellar. It had an escape tunnel at the north-east corner. Through this, he had hauled a seven-foot-square slab into the cellar, to act as a floor.

Now, Jason had returned, and he and his father pulled the body towards the hole. The whole family joined in, working as a team, pushing it into the depths; after the thump of its fall, the only sounds were the family's heaving breaths — and Jason's mocking laugh.

'You go down after supper,' he told his father. 'I think he has got plenty of money on him, and the boots and coat will be worth having. If we do not keep them we will sell them for a good profit in Independence, along with his horse.'

'*Ja.*' Old John gave his customary nod. In a day or two, he would dispose of the body, dragging it along the tunnel from the cellar.

Before she resumed her cooking, Ma Bender set about cleaning the place up, raking over the packed-earth floor, dragging the table back into place over the trapdoor. No point in arousing the suspicions of the next visitor. Blood had a nasty habit of smelling, if it wasn't attended to.

★ ★ ★

One day, Old Man Bender and his son Jason were returning in their wagon from Kansas City, where they had bought supplies for the inn. As rain began to fall, they found themselves in swampy ground. Father and son took shelter in a cave. They were shocked at what they found.

Through holes in the rock floor, hissing sounds emerged like the spitting of cats, and hot black fluid spurted upward.

'It's a mess in here,' Jason complained, expelling his plug of baccy. 'Stinks too!'

Old John didn't reply, but he stooped down and rubbed his hands in the viscous muck that darkened the floor.

Then he sniffed his hands.

'Oil,' he grunted, 'and something else.'

'What, Pappi?'

The old man lifted his nose into the air. 'Gas,' he said. And then he went into one of his silent moods, and it was clear his brain was ticking over. Presently Jason realized that the old man was getting really excited about something, but as they resumed their journey and eventually arrived back at the inn, they didn't talk about the cave.

The following week, father and son made another trip to Kansas City, and purchased a huge quantity of binder-twine and rope.

'What you want all that for, Pappi?' his son gasped.

His father just put on a mysterious expression and grunted, 'You will see.'

Over the next few weeks, Old John set the women to work fashioning a huge net from the twine — bigger than any fisherman's net they had ever seen. He also sent Almira out gathering quantities of milkweed leaves from the prairie, and these were crushed to produce sap. But this proved insufficient for the old man, and he supplemented his supply with twenty cans of gum from Kansas City, which he had stored in the back of the cave. Wicker was also collected, and he cut this into handy lengths ready for weaving. In addition, he had Katie make a dozen or so small sacks.

All he would say, when Katie pressed him about the purpose of this work, was, 'It will be our insurance. You will see.'

Almira smiled to herself. She knew what was in his mind.

★   ★   ★

The winter seemed to drag interminably, but finally it gave way to spring. Warmth banished the snow from the prairies. A profusion of sunflowers and other wild blooms coloured the landscape, and green wheat was shafting up in the cultivated sections. The Benders' apple-sprout orchard was growing healthily.

Over the past few weeks, several more wayfarers had mysteriously disappeared, and the trail from Osage Mission to Cherryvale was becoming notorious. A sixty-year old bachelor called Jasonny Boyle had set out to buy some land. He had $1900 on him at the time. Banks had not yet spread into the territory, and individuals tended to carry their money with them. In view of recent events, this was a foolhardy thing to do. Jasonny Boyle was never heard of again. The corpse of another man was found floating in the Verdigris River, but crawdads, catfish and snapping turtles had rendered him unrecognizable. A further body, with the skull crushed and throat cut, was found two weeks later in a waterhole four miles north of Oswego. Even though his eyes had been pecked out by buzzards, he was identified as 'a fella just travelling through'.

Concern had so heightened that

public meetings were held in all the local towns, and plans to form a vigilante group were drawn up. Suspicion swung towards several ranchers, but when their places were checked out, no incriminating evidence was found. Some folks suggested that renegade Osage Indians were guilty.

After a while, the name of Bender was mentioned, but people shied away from actually accusing the family. They figured if neighbours started blaming each other, the whole community would fall apart.

★   ★   ★

Old Man Bender was never idle these days. In the wagon, he had conveyed the great net and the wicker to the cave, storing it safely in the depths.

Jason had learned that in the old days, the Osage Indians had treated the cave as a place of evil spirits, because of the spitting sound that bubbled up from the floor and the terrible smell. In

49

consequence, the Indians had avoided it — and somehow its bad name had persisted even after the Osages had been shipped off to the reservation, and folks just didn't venture near the cave. When Jason mentioned this to his father, the old man grinned with satisfaction.

In due course, a great volume of silk was purchased in Kansas City. The family spent long hours at the cave, or just outside it to escape the obnoxious fumes. They worked in shifts, allowing one of them to remain at the inn and accommodate any customers who sought shelter. The Benders sewed the silk, weaving the wicker into a large basket, and nodding in acknowledgement as the old man instructed them. He was truly in his element. One day, he brought the auger to the cave and drilled down until he produced a vent and released an outpouring of gas. He plugged the hole with a wooden log, padded round with rags. He could easily unplug the hole, when the necessity arose.

5

It was in June of that year when Conroy McClure rode into the territory, looking for his twin brother who had gone missing five months earlier. Beside the trail, long slough grass swayed in the breeze.

A red-coloured poster caught Conroy's eye. It was displayed prominently, pinned to the trunk of a cottonwood tree. He pulled his piebald horse in close and scanned the printed words.

Prof. Miss KATIE BENDER
Can heal all sorts of diseases;
can cure Blindness,
Fits, and all such diseases,
Also Deaf and Dumbness.
Residence, 14 miles East of Independence, on the road from Independence to Osage Mission.

One and a half miles South-East of
Norahead Station.
KATIE BENDER

June 1872

Conroy decided to pay Katie Bender
a visit and ask about his brother. It was
worth a try, though would probably
provide the same negative results as his
search had produced so far. He would
call in to see her after he had stopped
off at the town of Cherryvale, *en route*.
He smiled to himself as he thought
that, if this woman was as clever as she
claimed, he might be able to get his
short stature attended to at the same
time. Lynching might do the trick, but
that wasn't an option he was considering.

Conroy, twenty-five years old, was
clad in a Stetson, dark blue hickory
shirt and well-worn buckskin pants.
The thing that set him apart from other
men was his lack of inches — he was
just five feet four inches tall — but he

tried to compensate for this by having large heels and soles fastened to his boots by wooden pegs. He'd had his footwear especially made, at no small cost. He and his brother Jesse ran a cattle-freighting company up north. Before that, the business had been owned by his father. But both father and mother had died as a result of a railroad accident, and everything had passed to the two boys, there being no other relatives of note. Conroy and Jesse had shared the business chores — at least they had done, until Jesse went missing.

His father had died instantly at the time of the accident, but his mother had lingered on for a few days in the hospital before the Grim Reaper had claimed her. Her last words haunted him. 'Look after Jesse. He's not so capable as you, Conroy. He's got to be taken care of.' Her hand had gripped his arm tightly, reflecting her intensity. 'Promise me!'

'Yes, Ma,' he'd nodded. 'I promise.'

His mother had leaned back with a satisfied sigh, and no doubt died believing she had done all she could, but his brother had made it extremely difficult for Conroy to keep his promise.

Strangely, for twin siblings, he and Jesse had never been close. In fact, quite the opposite, because an intense rivalry had developed between them, and Conroy had long concluded that Jesse's brain had been adversely affected at birth, giving him a jealous and suspicious nature. After the death of their parents, the twins had run the cattle freighting business together — or at least tried to. Jesse had accrued considerable gambling debts, had fleeced the business of most of its profits and, as his creditors pressed him, had walked out, leaving Conroy with only the briefest of notes. Hearing nothing for months, Conroy had eventually paid off his brother's debts, nigh crippling the business. He had sold up what limited assets remained. Then, bearing in mind the promise he had made, he'd set out to find Jesse, hoping that he might restore some stability to his brother's life. The trail had led him to Kansas; led him, unknowingly, towards horrendous danger.

★ ★ ★

Just after three that afternoon, Conroy reached the township of Cherryvale, passing the fine new Roman Catholic church. Black thunderclouds were building in the east, and the air smelt of rain. The town was bursting at the seams with hitched springboard wagons and horses. On enquiring, Conroy discovered that folks had come into town to attend a meeting at the Carpenter Schoolhouse. It had been called by a local politician, a Colonel Alexander York, a portly man who, Conroy was informed, had gained a name for himself as a tough fighter during the Civil War, and had commanded a regiment with distinction. Now, he was being talked about as a future senator.

Conroy shouldered his way into the crowded schoolhouse, anxious to hear what all the fuss was about. His ears pricked up when he heard that the gathering was to discuss the recent disappearance of folks in the district, the mutilated bodies found, and in particular, the disappearance of Colonel York's brother, Doctor William York. The medical man had been missing after paying the colonel a visit six weeks since. His wife had just announced that he had never returned home, having presumed he was still with his brother; otherwise, the searching would have started earlier.

Now, somebody recalled that they had spoken to the doctor just before he left Cherryvale, and he had said he was going to stop over at The Benders' Inn.

Conroy, standing at the back, listened to the various speakers, some of whom shouted with anger. The whole throng was blazing mad.

A claim-by-claim search had been

carried out in the territory, including streams and waterholes, and Colonel York expounded how convinced he was that the Bender family was behind the trouble.

Conroy recalled the name of the girl on the poster: Katie Bender. She must be a member of the self-same family.

Colonel York said a group of vigilantes should be raised to administer justice. And now men kept repeating the name of Bender, and their faces reddened, and somebody shouted that they should rip the Bender claim apart until they found evidence. If proof of skulduggery were found, the inn should be burned, with the Benders still in it! Other folks were keener on outright lynching, so as to be sure none of the guilty escaped. Conroy figured that if anybody with the name Bender had been present here at the schoolhouse, they would have been strung up straight away.

As Colonel York sat down, a man with droopy eyelids stood up and raised his hands to quiet the racket of angry voices. When he spoke, his moustache resembled a caterpillar crawling under his nose.

When he at last could make himself heard, he said, 'As Town Trustee, I hereby propose that we elect Colonel York as chairman of the vigilantes, and having done that we make up a posse of fifty or so men to bring justice to the guilty parties.'

'Seconded!' somebody else yelled.

'All agreed?' the Town Trustee demanded, and was drowned out by assenting voices.

However, some men later stated they couldn't hit the trail until they'd attended to their livestock and tied up matters at home. Cows had to be milked regardless, and chickens fed, but they would come as quickly as they could.

Conroy McClure decided it was time to leave, and backed out of the schoolhouse. He had the feeling that the Bender family wouldn't get much chance for talking once the vigilantes got hold of them. It seemed that everybody had made up their minds that they were guilty, further proof or not. He desperately wanted to establish the fate of his own brother before all those who knew, and all evidence, were destroyed, possibly by incineration. He hurriedly returned to his piebald horse, unhitched him and swung into the saddle.

Nobody paid him any attention as he set out along the Old Osage Mission trail, raking his mount for speed with the blunted rowels of his spurs. As he rode, the brightness disappeared from the sky and thunder rumbled. Several times his horse reared up, frightened by tumbleweed swirling across the trail, caught in the bullying wind.

A possibility hastened him. If the Benders somehow got word of the way suspicion was swinging in their direction, they might well hightail out of the territory, disappearing as effectively as their alleged victims.

He kept his piebald mount at a relentless pace, stopping only once to pull on his poncho as protection from raindrops, now falling as large as well-chewed wads of tobacco. He passed through several sections of fenced-off land, saw a number of homesteads, but eventually these vanished as the trail became more remote. The day was fading into shadowless gloom.

He figured he was some three or four miles from Osage Mission when he spotted a large mound of rocks showing black against the sky, and shortly he saw a pin-point of lantern-light coming from a cabin, surrounded by some outbuildings and a pole-corral, all standing about a hundred yards back from the trail. He guessed this was The Benders' Inn.

Drawing up, he gave his intentions a moment's thought. The place looked downright spooky, up there on its slight hill, and he had no wish to stick his neck into a noose, but some strange premonition warned him that the explanation of his brother's fate lay there. The scene seemed even more sinister as lightning stabbed across the sky, followed closely by thunder. He fumbled beneath his poncho to check his Peacemaker Colt. The feel of the wooden grip was reassuring. He snapped the loading gate closed, making sure that a loaded chamber was under the firing pin and that the weapon rested easily in its holster, then he heeled his animal up the slope.

6

As he drew closer, he saw the sign above the doorway: GROCERIES.

He reined in his piebald, and the cabin's door opened, allowing lantern light to silhouette the figure that appeared. This seemed more like a great bear than a human being. A great bear wearing tattered overalls.

Conroy swallowed his apprehension and said, 'Howdy. I hear you provide good food and a bed here.'

'*Ja*,' Old John Bender muttered gruffly, his bearded face as expressionless as a red hatchet. '*Mein sohn* Jason . . . he take your horse.'

Conroy nodded and swung from his saddle. 'Sure is the devil's weather we're getting,' he said, but the old man did not answer, seeming not to hear.

A younger man stepped out from the cabin. He was well built and very tall, towering over Conroy. His eyes were so close-set they seemed to constrict the bridge of his nose. As he took the reins from Conroy, he emitted a laugh, revealing crooked teeth. Conroy wondered what he found so funny, unless it was the prospect of another easy victim. The Bender son smoothed the wet flank of the piebald with his hand, as if appraising it. He made an appreciative sound with his lips. It was then that he swung back, perhaps getting his first clear look at Conroy's face — and he made a sudden, weird click in his throat. The blood had drained from his face. He turned away sharply, leading the horse off.

Uneasily, Conroy followed the great bulk of the old man through the cabin doorway, and the smell of staleness assailed him. A black-garbed woman, built like a pickle barrel, greeted him with a nod, but didn't speak or smile. She helped him off with his poncho. She then shook the rain out of it and hung it on the hook behind the door.

It was at this moment that Conroy saw Katie Bender for the first time.

She had stepped from behind the calico curtain that partitioned the room, wiping her hands on her apron, her face illuminated by the candle she was holding. There was a touch of rouge on her cheeks. She suddenly smiled. Conroy was astonished by her beauty. Everything else about this place was as ugly as abomination, yet the appearance of this auburn-haired woman was somehow breathtaking. He noted the rounded curves of her hips beneath her wool challis dress and, lifting his gaze, met the disturbing, wanton force that inhabited the depths of her eyes.

'Mister,' she said, 'if you want homely comforts, you have certainly come to the right place.' She glanced at the older woman. 'Can we prepare some food for this gentleman, Motti?'

Almira Bender nodded and stepped behind the curtain. The rattle of pans was soon emanating from that direction.

For a moment nobody said anything.

Conroy felt that the walls were tight around him, enclosing him in a snare that so many others might well have fallen victim to. Had his brother Jesse been treated with equal hospitality? And yet one question troubled him. In view of the fact that he and his twin brother were identical and had been mistaken for each other many times, the Bender family had not shown any surprise at his appearance, when the natural reaction might have been that 'he had returned from the dead'. That is, apart from the strange look that Jason had given him when he'd taken his horse. Did *that* have any significance?

Of course there was another possibility. In spite of the unsavoury nature of Old Man Bender and his family, they might be as innocent as lambs, and their accusers from Cherryvale and elsewhere might be wrong in their damning assumptions.

The girl intrigued him. Perhaps Katie Bender was as angelic as her smiling face indicated. Her green eyes hadn't left his from the time he'd stepped inside the cabin. The thought of such a beautiful creature falling foul of rough-handed, biased and hoary men, burning with lust for vengeance, was momentarily abhorrent to him.

'Make yourself at home,' she said. 'Take the seat against the curtain. We call that our place of honour. Motti is making a lovely stew for tonight.'

He nodded, slid on to the bench where she pointed. Behind him, beyond the curtain, the roar of Mrs Bender's cook-stove sounded. Old John Bender had joined her.

Katie was suddenly alongside him, closer than you'd have expected after such short acquaintance.

'A girl gets lonely out here,' she murmured, in a soft tone. The Teutonic edge on her voice gave it an undeniable seductiveness, despite the fact she tried to speak 'easy' American.

'You're not from this way?' she said. 'I have not seen you before.'

'I'm from up north, Montana. I'm in the cattle-freighting business.'

'Sounds interesting.' She nodded. 'Must be quite profitable.'

'We've done pretty well.' He was anxious to draw her out, to glean any information he could. 'I came down this way to conduct some business.'

'I thought you had.' She smiled. Her body was so close that he could feel her curves, her yielding femininity, almost as if she were naked beneath her dress. It was strange how the pressure of a woman's flesh was so different from anything else, how it caused the blood to throb through a man's veins and have his manhood develop a will of its own.

She had felt something, too: the bulge of the money-belt under his shirt.

'I guessed you were an astute businessman,' she said, and laughed gently.

He edged her away from the subject, pretending that her nearness was of no consequence. 'I'm looking for my twin brother,' he said. 'He came this way about five months ago. Haven't seen him since. I wonder if you came across him.'

'We do get folk passing through,' she said. 'What was his name?'

'Jesse McClure. He would've probably stayed overnight.'

She shook her head, making her hair glisten in the candlelight. 'Jesse McClure. The name doesn't sound familiar. If he was like you, I'd sure remember.' She rested her hand on his. 'Say, mister, the rain's eased off. Why don't we take a stroll down to the orchard? More private down there. Motti won't have the meal fixed for a moment or two.'

He felt an urge to be outside; fresh air might soothe his jangling senses.

'That'd be good,' he said, and he stood up. A sense of foolishness assailed him, for he had forgotten how vulnerable he'd been with his back against the curtain.

A moment later and she had led him outside. True enough the rain had stopped, but the premature darkness remained. Everywhere was damp underfoot, but the air was refreshed and the blossom from the apple trees perfumed the evening.

'You sure you ain't seen my brother?' he enquired.

She nodded her head. 'Sure as can be.'

'You lived in these parts long, Katie?'

'A couple of years or so. Before that, we were in Tennessee. We did a spot of baby-farming.'

'Baby-farming?' he queried.

'Sure. We used to buy in orphan babies, fatten them up and sell them at good profit. The older ones we trained to pick pockets.'

He exhaled sharply at her outrageousness and she laughed.

'You're so easily shocked,' she said. 'You believe anything!'

'So, it's not true?'

'Well, yes, I guess so. That was when we first came over from Germany. But I got sick of all those squawking brats, and it got too expensive, dosing them with liquor, so we moved down here and opened up the inn. Pappi and Motti still haven't picked up the language too well. Way back in Germany, Pappi was a balloon-seamster. He used to make them air balloons that people go up in. I remember how he made one, all by himself. Took us on a ride right across the country. I recall floating up and up, as if we were on the way to Heaven. It was beautiful, truly beautiful. I felt like an angel.'

Her hand had slipped into his. They stepped over ground that was decidedly uneven. Alongside an apple tree, they stopped and were enshrouded with the sweetest scent. She faced him. 'Like I said, it gets really lonely for a girl here. You are the first *real* man that's passed by for an age. A girl gets so hungry for a kiss.'

The closeness of her lips, her beautiful face, gazing at him pleadingly, was tempting. He felt that he was Adam, and this was his Eve, here in the apple orchard. He drew her into him, and she enjoyed it and rubbed her breasts against his chest. He pressed his lips to hers, felt the yielding sweetness of her body, but then he recalled how easy it would be for somebody to creep up behind him and club him down, perhaps her awesome brother, and he disentangled himself from her.

'I'm starving,' he announced, sensing her annoyance. 'I guess your ma's got the food ready by now.'

She grabbed his arm. 'Just when I was getting stirred up!' she exclaimed. 'I will tell you something,' she said, 'I always get what I want.'

'And right now, you want . . . ?'

'You, honey.'

And he felt she really meant it.

7

Almira Bender's stew consisted of nothing more exotic than tough, stringy meat and beans. Once again, Conroy was obliged to position himself in the so-called place of honour, with his back against the curtain, but while the family were seated at the table around him, he felt reasonably safe. He was confident he could defend himself if he had to. And with them all spooning their stew from the same dish, there seemed little likelihood of any attempt being made to poison him.

He wondered if and when the vigilantes would appear. That Colonel York had seemed a pretty dedicated sort of fellow. If he was intent on doing something, it seemed mighty clear that he would. Maybe they'd try to burn the place down during the night. Conroy reasoned he best stay awake.

The family seemed uncommonly quiet as far as words were concerned, not even conversing in German. The old man ladled stew into his mouth, not caring that half of it ran down into his rat's-nest beard. His wife kept her eyes down. Jason picked stringy meat from his crooked teeth with long black fingernails and frequently eyed Conroy. And Katie seemed right pleased with herself, giving Conroy secret smiles between every dainty mouthful.

Conroy gazed around the place. The only light now came from flickering candles. He finished his meal and moved away from the vulnerable position close to the curtain.

Outside the cabin, night had closed in, black as the inside of a cow's belly. Inside, Old John and his wife spread the mattresses on the floor, on both sides of the curtain, choosing themselves to sleep out of view, in the kitchen section. It seemed that both Jason and his sister intended to sleep behind the counter, leaving Conroy to the front section. At least he felt he was positioned close to the door and that the chance of escape was near at hand, should the necessity arise.

Individually, the family vacated the cabin, no doubt to use the privy behind the property, if there was one. Conroy chose to relieve himself beyond the orchard. He stayed out as long as he could without arousing suspicion, wandering through the orchard and shadowy outhouses. In the dark barn, he discovered his piebald horse, tethered. She whickered to him softly. He understood the language she spoke. Right now she was hungry, and he suspected that she had not been given any oats, but there was nothing he could do about it. Come morning, he would make sure she had a good feed.

Everywhere seemed pretty run down and decrepit, and a strong stench came from the hog-pen. He found nothing untoward in the shadowy gloom, apart from the undulations in the ground of the orchard. The thought crossed his mind that here might be the graves of the folk who had disappeared — even his own brother. He shuddered, and knew that in the now moonless darkness he would be unable to determine anything. The air was humid and heavy, and he was sure more rain was on the way.

When he returned to the cabin, he opened the door quietly and slid the latch back into place. Soundlessly, he walked to the mattress that had been assigned for his use, and lowered himself on to it, choosing not to use the blanket provided, as he suspected it was full of fleas and lice. From behind the curtain came the sound of the old man's snoring. Sometimes he'd inhale a great gulp of air, go quiet for a moment, then resume snoring with a splutter. Conroy figured the snoring was a good sign. At least his host was not plotting murder, or apparently not.

Conroy had spent a long time on the trail that day, and he was weary, but he was determined to stay alert; however, his intentions were thrown into disarray by the girl. Scarcely had he rested his head down, when a faint movement disturbed him and he heard her soft laugh.

'I heard tell,' she whispered, 'that the bed of a lonely man is never warm. Move over. I think you might like a little company.'

He hesitated, but his resolve diminished as the musky female scent of Katie Bender touched his nostrils. It was said the best way to learn a foreign language was from a bedmate; maybe he might yet be able to glean something about his brother from the girl. As he moved to make room for her on the mattress and she slipped alongside him, he discovered that she was completely naked, and despite his good intentions, he felt his breath quicken. Like a hundred-and-ten per cent of the male population in that territory, he was woman-hungry, and the fears that this temptress might have served the same delights to others who were now in their graves had momentarily left his mind, as did the thought that the blanket she pulled over them might be seething with livestock.

'Honey,' she whispered in his ear, 'do you always sleep with your boots on?'

'Sure,' he responded, 'but I've taken off my spurs.'

He felt her fingers fumbling with his belt, unfastening the buckle, and thereupon she encountered what lay beneath — his money-belt. But she made no comment and turned her attention to unbuttoning his shirt, slipping her hand amidst the hair of his chest.

'I love hairy men,' she murmured mischievously, and then he felt her fingers inching downwards, inside his trousers, finding his manhood. Again she laughed. 'For a small man, honey, you are uncommonly large down here!'

He groaned at her touch. He ran his hands across her warm breasts, touching the firmness of her nipples, feeling the excitement throbbing through her body.

It was then that he realized a dark bulk was looming over them, reaching down to lift the blanket. The girl reacted immediately.

'Vamoose, Jason! It is not your turn tonight.'

'Katie, I thought . . . '

'Well, you thought wrong. Anyway, it was Pappi's turn tonight, and he is not complaining.'

Jason emitted a mean sigh and dissolved back into the darkness.

Conroy could hardly believe his ears. His hands remained cupping her breasts. 'You mean your old man and brother take turns with you?'

She laughed. 'Sure, honey. I do not know why you sound so shocked. Most of the boys in Kansas have it off with their sisters. How do you think I keep Pappi and my no-good brother so obedient? They know that if they don't do as they're told, they won't get their nookie!'

He gasped with disbelief.

The intervention of Jason had interfered with her flow of action. It had also reminded him that he had allowed his guard to drop. Jason could have shot him, or slipped a knife into him.

'Say,' she whispered, 'could you take off your gun? It gets in the way . . . and maybe your boots? It would be so much more intimate without them. Our toes could snuggle up to each other, I mean.'

He pondered on her request. 'I'll take the gun off, not the boots,' he conceded.

He slid the Peacemaker from its holster, and rested it on the floor, alongside the mattress. It was ready-primed. All he had to do, in an emergency, was reach out and grab it.

'Oh, well,' Katie sighed, 'keep your boots on if you must. A girl can't have everything she wants, but I did not keep a stitch on myself.'

'I noticed that, Katie.' He allowed himself a laugh. 'You come on top. You're such a delicate flower. I wouldn't want to squash you.'

The truth was, he figured he could

use her as a shield if they were interrupted again — but gradually, as his passions took over, and the girl's hands were under his clothes, finding spots where he hadn't been caressed for far too long, he knew she was hotter than any hired woman he'd experienced. She guided him into her with an exuberance that made clear she was not faking, crying out as they pumped each other, not giving a damn whether the rest of the family heard or not.

When he came, she was totally orgasmic, acting like a crazy woman.

'Again, honey!' she panted. 'Again and again!'

It is true to say that over the next hour, Conroy forgot the danger he was in, forgot that the vigilantes might burst upon the place at any second with flaming torches and blazing guns. He overlooked that there was anybody else in the world beyond this woman who had feasted upon his body with such abandoned delight.

Afterwards, deep into the night, she

lay in his arms, warm and seemingly sated. 'That was lovely,' she murmured. 'Truly lovely. I have never known a man like you.'

'I guess women like Katie Bender don't come round too often, either,' he remarked. He added 'Thank God' beneath his breath, so she could not hear.

'I have always said this was the best inn in Kansas,' she said, her lips touching the lobe of his ear. 'But the customers have got to be of the right disposition.'

He felt her hand snake down across his belly, circumnavigate his money-belt, then descend to his manhood.

'You got everything a customer needs,' she whispered. 'Now, this girl is tired. Let us get some sleep. There's work to do in the morning.'

You bet there is, he thought.

8

Conroy didn't sleep. He lay awake, comforted by the feel of the naked girl in his arms and the soft music of her breathing, despite the undercurrent of uneasiness that swirled through his innards. He was also conscious that the rain had returned, causing a steady thump against the cabin's roof. Maybe the rain would cool the hot blood of the vigilantes, but he doubted it.

Gradually, common sense returned to him. Somehow he knew that Katie had not been putting on an act with her overwhelming passion, and neither had he, but he still reckoned she would sanction his murder when the time came. And how many more men had she welcomed in this way? The answer might rest beneath the uneven soil of the orchard.

He was on his feet as soon as he

heard the old man's stirring and breaking wind from behind the curtain. He buttoned up his clothing, reached down, retrieved the Peacemaker and slipped it into its holster. Shortly, a crackle of fat sounded and the aroma of frying bacon pervaded the cabin.

He gazed down at the girl in the faint morning light. Half of a second mattress was dragged across her nudity, leaving only one breast peeping out, but she still looked downright beautiful.

'You like my sister, mister?'

Conroy turned and saw Jason rising from his mattress, tucking his shirt into the top of his trousers, laughing in the unnerving way he had.

'I like her,' Conroy said, 'but my horse doesn't seem to care for the accommodation. I figure he could do with some oats.'

'Oh *ja*, mister. I'll see to that. Can't have any dissatisfaction around here, not even from a horse.' He turned to face Conroy full on.

'I guess you might have seen

somebody *like* me before,' he said.

'*Nein*,' Jason responded, and turned away.

Conroy raised the latch and opened the cabin door, glad of the fresh air that wafted to him. He stepped outside, stood beneath the sullen sky. He chose not to turn his back on the cabin, figuring he didn't want to be caught unawares by a quick bullet or knife-thrust. Now, more than ever, he was convinced that his twin brother had come this way. Depression settled over him. Could be he would never honour that promise he had made to his mother as she died.

It was raining quite hard. He gazed down towards the Cherryvale trail, wondering if Colonel York had rounded up his vigilantes, but there was no sign of them.

It occurred to him that he could hightail out of this place here and now, and no doubt save himself a lot of trouble, but he had upon him the sense of a job not completed. The Benders were obviously an unsavoury bunch, though he assured himself that the girl was different from the others. He wondered if the outrageous things she'd said had been made up and merely intended to shock him. Even so, the prospect of being with her for a while longer appealed to him. He would remember the night of passion he had spent with her until the end of his life — whether that came from natural causes or otherwise.

When he returned to the cabin, the household was a-bustle, and Almira Bender was dishing up the breakfast. Katie was busy setting the table with knives, spoons and forks, a jug of milk and a loaf of bread. She gave him a wild smile and her lips moved as she whispered words he didn't catch, but suspected were some lewd reference to the intimacy they had shared during the night.

She gestured to 'the place of honour', and he sat on the bench with his back to the curtain. But he remained alert, determined to leap to the side the instant he suspected violence. It was not a situation entirely conducive to satisfactory digestion.

'Breakfast smells good,' Katie remarked, slipping in alongside him.

Her mother appeared, coming around the curtain with a platter of sizzling bacon. He wondered where the old man and his son were. Then he heard the slightest of movements from behind the curtain, and anger rose in him, anger that he had placed himself in such a vulnerable position.

But Katie screeched, 'No, Pappi! Not yet!'

Instinctively, he leaned forward. He glanced at Katie, saw how the warmth had left her features to be replaced by sudden fear.

But the girl's words didn't sink into the old man's blood-hazed brain. Conroy attempted to throw himself to the side, but he was too late to avoid the slamming blow from the hammer. It caught the side of his skull, leaving an ugly red groove and sending him reeling to the floor, where he lay briefly writhing. His breath was coming in heavy surges, his body shuddering like a clubbed fish. Suddenly his breathing subsided.

'I said not to do it, you fool!' Katie sobbed out. 'This one was different.'

John Bender had appeared, gripping his knife, but Almira impeded him as she stooped over the body, ripping open the shirt. Her plump, greedy fingers grabbed hold of the money-belt, unfastened the buckle and pulled it off.

Old John watched lickerishly, his mouth gaping like a black egg. His wife opened the purse and clawed out the contents. But the result was not what she had expected. Just two dollar coins, some old paper and assorted rubbish appeared in her hand.

'*Mein Gotte!*' she howled. 'I thought he had money on him!'

The old man was cursing in German, and Katie had clutched her apron to her face in shock. This wasn't what she'd intended.

'Maybe in his pockets,' Almira gasped, and she was about to rummage when her son shouted from outside.

'Somebody comes!'

The three Benders rushed to the open doorway and saw that a single rider was approaching from the trail.

'Clean up the place!' Katie shouted at her mother. She was furious that her slow-witted father had clubbed down this lover who had shown ardour far beyond anything she'd ever previously encountered. She knew she had left matters too late. She should have realized that once her father was set in a line of action, nothing would retard him.

'Make sure there's no blood!' she snapped at him. 'And put his body into the cellar . . . and be quick, you stupid old mule.'

She dragged the table aside, fumbled with the trapdoor and drew it open. Meanwhile, Old John had gripped

Conroy beneath the armpits, dragged him over the black hole, and dropped him unceremoniously into the depths. Within a moment the trapdoor was closed and the table was drawn back into place.

The old man didn't want his daughter to be all stirred up again, so he didn't mention the fact that the stranger had still been breathing.

9

Feisty Aaron Simmons, a horse-doctor from Cherryvale, had despaired at the slowness with which the vigilantes were acting, and, having fortified himself with apple-whiskey, had decided to ride out to the inn and check on the Benders for himself.

On arrival, he did not go directly to the cabin, but drew off to the side so as to inspect the orchard. To a casual observer, the bumps in the ground would have aroused little excitement, but to the suspicious eye of Simmons they immediately attracted attention. Dismounting from his horse, he placed his clumpy feet carefully in the oozing mud. Soon, he was stooping beside a spot that was particularly uneven. He could see where the earth had settled into a rectangular-shaped depression. Rainwater made it particularly evident.

It was the size of a man's body. He found a stick and had started to scrape away the muddy soil, when he encountered the pallid whiteness of a human hand. Decaying flesh hung from the fingers in shreds. He grunted with disgust. He scraped the soil back into place, and was rising to his stumpy legs when he heard the hawk and discharge of a tobacco plug from a man's throat and realized he wasn't alone.

'What you sniffing about for, Mister Fat Man?'

Simmons spun around to find himself gazing into the muzzle-end of a .50 calibre Sharps rifle. Gripping the gun, Jason Bender was looming over him like a predatory hawk.

Simmons unleashed a growl of annoyance, then said, 'Colonel York and his vigilantes will have some questions to ask you when I tell him what I've found. They'll be here mighty soon.'

Jason emitted a scornful laugh. 'One thing's certain: you are not going to tell anybody!' And his narrow-set eyes had taken on a maniacal glint.

Simmons had no time to respond.

Jason's finger tightened on the trigger and the gun blasted off, blowing a bloody hole in the visitor's chest.

★ ★ ★

Jason returned to the cabin, shaking his head and smiling to himself.

'What have you done, you fool?' Katie demanded.

'That fellow who came. He said Colonel York and some vigilantes were coming out here. He was digging into the graves in the orchard, uncovered a bit of body, so I killed him. No point in him spreading word.'

'Then it's time we moved on,' Katie acknowledged. 'We must get out of here quick. I do not fancy getting strung up.'

'I was just thinking the same thing,' he nodded. 'I do not think our business has any future here now.'

She shot her father a meaningful glance and Old John grunted something and hurried out of the cabin. Her mother started to pull together a few things.

Katie turned to her brother. 'You go back to the orchard and hide that man's body. There is no point in advertising to all and sundry what you've done.'

'I have already. I am not stupid, Katie.'

The Benders had few possessions of value, apart from the big leather satchel that Katie now dragged from the clapboard closet. It was heavier than she anticipated. It contained the cash they'd stolen since they'd started operations at the inn — nearly $50,000. They certainly wouldn't be short of cash when they departed.

A half hour later, Old Man Bender returned, indicating that all was ready for them to take flight. Katie had suspected that this moment would come, all the while they'd lived here, and she was glad that her father had completed the preparations meticulously. But she knew they weren't safe yet.

Suddenly there was a shattering of glass accompanied by the echoing blast of a gun. Jason let out a shout of agony and slumped to the floor in an untidy heap, blood flowing fast from his right shoulder, staining his shirt. A bullet had passed clean through him and gone out through the timber of the far wall.

Katie shrieked with horror, but as she stooped over her brother, a voice boomed from outside, coming with the resonance of thunder.

'All you Benders, come out with your hands up! There are fifty men here. You got two minutes. If you don't come out, we'll burn your place to the ground, and you with it!'

Old John risked a look through the shattered window and unleashed a coarse German oath. He could see vigilantes, looking like black ants as they swarmed up from the trail towards the cabin, shouting as they came. Most of them had guns. One had a blazing torch.

Jason was scrambling shakily to his

feet, bloody fingers gripping his shoulder. For once the sly laugh was absent from him, replaced by a grimace of pain. He had fallen heavily, on to the point where the bullet had entered. Blood was pumping out of him, but nobody paid him much attention.

Katie had moved the table back from the trapdoor and opened up the cellar. 'Come on,' she shrieked. 'For God's sake, be quick!'

Almira Bender led the way, drawing up her skirts and clambering down through the hole, showing surprising agility considering her bulk. She'd been in tight situations before, and was never averse to beating a hasty retreat when appropriate. Old John followed, and then Katie kicked her brother into motion, goading him across the floor and forcing him down, regardless of his groans. She turned back, gathered up the heavy satchel containing their ill-gotten fortune, and dropped it into the cellar. Stooping, she paused to pull the table back into position and then lowered herself, stood on the stepladder and dragged the trapdoor closed above her head. She had practised it many times before.

She hoped that the vigilantes would keep to their word and burn the place to ash. By that time, the family could be well away. But if the vigilantes chose to storm the cabin, they would be met by no resistance and it wouldn't take Colonel York long to discover how the family had escaped.

The gas-like stench in the tiny cellar was overpowering, but the Benders were used to it. For a moment they blundered against each other in the darkness. Jason was doubled over, constantly cursing and groaning with pain, and the old man shouted at him to shut up. Almira had brought a lantern, and she scraped sulphur and dim light flooded through the gloom. Her husband swore as he stumbled over the sprawled frame of Conroy McClure. He had forgotten about him, but now, despite their desperation, greed took hold of him.

'The money,' he grunted to Katie. 'You said he had money.'

'No time,' Katie snapped back. 'We have got plenty in the satchel. We must get out now.'

But Old John ignored her and stooped over Conroy's prostrate form, roughly checking his pockets and blaspheming with anger, as he discovered nothing of value.

In the flickering light of the lantern, they stood nonplussed. At last, Katie said, 'Those boots. The heels are so big. Perhaps that is why he didn't take the boots off when he went to bed. Maybe he's got cash stacked away in the heels.'

Old John's eyes gleamed with delight, seizing on to the suggestion with alacrity. He grabbed Conroy's left leg, tugged at the boot, but it was slippery with blood and Conroy's foot seemed arched, as if some innate stubbornness was preventing him from having his boots stolen.

'My God!' Katie exclaimed. 'He's

still breathing.' She felt a strange inner satisfaction at this discovery. She'd never felt this way before about anybody.

'He will not be alive for long,' Almira said.

The old man's excitement had changed to fury. 'I'll cut his leg off!' he yelled.

Katie shouted, 'There's no time, you fool. We must get away! We'll have to take him with us.'

Old John growled with displeasure, started to argue, but she screamed at him to hold his tongue.

From above their heads came the sound of more shots being fired into the cabin, rattling the timbers, and the angry shouting of the attackers set the Benders into movement.

Old John grabbed Conroy's small frame beneath the armpits and hoisted him on to his great back, and the whole family crawled through the opening into the narrow earthiness of the tunnel, Almira holding the kerosene lamp high, sending crazy shadows dancing about them. Conroy's back sometimes scraped against the low roof, bringing down a shower of earth, but Old John didn't pause, and Jason brought up the rear, his shirt made bloody as he clutched his shoulder, his curses coming in a constant stream.

10

Colonel York and his vigilantes advanced on the cabin like the skirmish line of a military formation, their assortment of guns at the ready. They moved with their heads ducked down in case a fusillade of shots erupted from the window. York had decided against burning the place down, in case vital evidence was destroyed. Nearing the entrance, he signalled a halt, and his men went to ground, their weapons trained on the window and door.

The whole place seemed deadly quiet, and the rain was dripping down relentlessly, thumping on to the roof.

Colonel York cupped his hands to his mouth and raised his voice into the hush. 'This is your last chance to come out with your hands up! If we come in to get you, we won't be taking no prisoners.'

Everybody held their breath, listening for some response, but none came and Colonel York cursed. His patience was running out. Somebody behind him yelled, 'Let's get 'em!', and there were shouts of agreement.

The colonel gestured the mob forward, leading the surge, his finger on his trigger. Reaching the inn door, he hesitated, then kicked it. It took two further kicks before the door gave. The colonel dodged to the side to avoid the possible deluge of bullets, but none came, and seconds later men were crowding into the room, ripping aside the curtain and swearing with frustration as they found the place deserted.

An initial search revealed little of value, apart from three hammers, an eight-day clock and a German Bible. But as the colonel searched the cupboard, he discovered a bridle and a pair of spectacles, and, with a sinking heart, he realized that they had belonged to his brother.

He ordered his men to investigate the outbuildings.

All they discovered were six half-starved hogs, some scraggy poultry and three hungry horses in the barn, including a piebald mare.

One of the colonel's sidekicks said, 'I seen that piebald before. I seed it in town being ridden by a fella who attended the meeting at the school-house, when we was deciding what to do about the Benders.'

'Then you figure he warned them we were coming?' York asked.

'Could be.'

Another man shouted, 'Well, he deserves lynching alongside the Benders!'

Colonel York had carried on looking around the cabin. He noticed that the old table was standing at a strange angle, and he went to it and dragged it aside. That was when he saw the trapdoor in the floor. He reached down, grasped the strap-handle and tentatively eased it open. The smell surged into the room like a burst of poisonous gas. It was foul, and had men coughing and spluttering.

At that moment somebody called from outside that a body had been found in the adjacent orchard. It belonged to Aaron Simmons!

Colonel York let the trapdoor fall shut and led the way outside, glad enough to escape the stench, down to where a crowd of men had gathered amid the apple saplings. Some had found shovels and were digging into the earth. Some used wagon rods to poke into the mounds.

There must have been nigh a hundred men crowding around the Bender claim by then. Word had somehow got around, and folks were arriving on foot, in oxcarts, wagons and buckboards, and riding horses. A reporter from the *Leavenworth Times* was busy scribbling notes. The cabin rapidly became a complete mess, with everybody tramping around. Mr Leroy Dick, the droopy-eyed town trustee, was bossing men in a loud voice.

As earth was turned in the orchard, the atmosphere became polluted with foul air. Men dug carefully, knowing that they would shortly be digging up corpses.

The first body discovered was face down with legs bent back. The skull had been crushed, and as the body was turned over, everybody saw how the throat had been cut so deeply that the head had nearly come away. It was a sickening sight, and Colonel York's face became set like solid stone and his lips were trembling as he said, 'That's my brother, William. God rest his soul!'

Over the next hour, more bodies were dug up. Eleven in all, nine males and two females. Each, except one, had been killed in the same way: the back of the head smashed in and the throat cut. The exception was a little blonde-headed girl of about ten. She was found in the same grave as her father, her hands hugging him around the waist. There wasn't a sign of a blow on her, so she must have been thrown in after her father and smothered to death as the earth was piled in. Later, the man was identified as the freshly widowed George Loncher, who was taking his daughter to stay with her grandparents in Iowa.

Most of the bodies were virtually naked, the clothes having been stolen from their backs. One of them was so badly cut up, that it was impossible to tell whether it was male or female.

One man yelled out, 'By God, we'll hunt these monsters down, even if they've run to the ends of the earth!', and tears were running down his cheeks, just as they were running down everybody else's cheeks when that little girl was laid upon the ground.

'If anybody around here was in cahoots with them hyenas, we'll hunt them down as well, and lynch 'em, by Christ!'

'Yeah, we'll make cottonwood blossoms of 'em all.'

Feelings were running so high that

anger was turned on Rudolph Brockman, who lived on the nearest claim to the Benders' inn. He was disliked by many, and had a reputation for being cruel to animals. Also, he was known to speak German. Now he was accused of being in league with the murderers. In next to no time, a rope was around his neck, and had Colonel York, with his ambitions towards becoming a senator, not intervened, the poor man would have gone to his maker. In the event, the noose was removed and Brockman rapidly vacated the scene.

There was a general reluctance to climb down into the inn's cellar — the stench was downright evil — so some long poles were found and pushed beneath the cabin. Straining hard, men forced the cabin aside and exposed the cellar, disturbing a great cloud of flies.

The smell lifted about them so nauseatingly that several men backed off and vomited.

The cellar proved to be empty, but the stone-slab floor was covered with stains, and around the dirt edges a considerable amount of blood had coagulated. It was this that caused the stench. A local doctor confirmed it was human blood.

Quite a few women had now appeared from town, and many of them had entered the Benders' cabin. Everybody wanted souvenirs. Some of them carried out the mattresses. Soon, the place was stripped bare. Everybody wanted something to prove that they had been part of that day. By the next morning, they had torn the cabin apart, carrying off the boards and logs and stones, and even the apple saplings. There wasn't a single thing left on the property to show that the inn had ever been there, except the gaping hole which had been the cellar.

But where were the Benders?

11

Katie considered it weird — sitting in the back of a wagon with two bodies sprawled beside her, both more dead than alive. In fact, between her brother and Conroy, she wouldn't have taken bets as to who would expire first. But she found herself praying that Conroy would survive. She would never forget the previous night, and the passion he had created in her. She had never known anything like it — and it had hurt her almost as much as it had Conroy when her father's hammer had descended, or so she reckoned. The old man had acted with unwarranted impetuousness.

On the front seat of the wagon, alongside Almira, Katie's father was driving at ferocious speed, whipping the two horses mercilessly. The terrain often lacked a recognized trail, just rugged ground that was jolting them all to Hell. Yet the way was familiar to them, for they had covered it a hundred times before as they had come to work in the cave.

Something that troubled Old John was the fact that his wagon had an unusual positioning of the wheels, the front wheels being at narrower width than the rear ones. It would thus be easier for any pursuers to pick up the trail. He wished he had paid attention to this fact long ago, but he had only recently realized the wagon's uniqueness. So far, he had seen no sign of anybody coming after them, but he was certain that Colonel York would strike up the trail soon enough. His mind swung to Conroy McClure. Maybe it was him who had led the vigilantes to suspect that the Bender family had been running a 'business' from their inn. Old John growled with anger. If Conroy wasn't dead already, he would make him pay dearly for his treachery, but right now, it was obvious that vigilantes or bounty hunters would show up soon, and he was unwilling to delay.

Almira Bender had glanced over her shoulder at her son Jason, her heart filled with a compassion she had seldom shown. 'Dear God,' she cried, 'I think he's gone!'

Old John cursed, and hauled on the reins, bringing the wagon to a jolting halt.

But as they gazed at Jason, he emitted a grunt and opened his narrow-set eyes. His mouth sagged open, a trickle of blood showing at the side of his lips.

'I am dying,' he groaned. 'I cannot go on. You must leave me. Rest me down where I can die in peace. I cannot stand this jolting any more.'

'We cannot leave you, son.' His mother seemed close to tears. 'It would not be Christian.'

Old Man Bender opened his mouth, but didn't say anything. Katie seemed more interested in fussing over Conroy.

'For God's sake, leave me,' Jason pleaded.

His father gazed back along the way they'd come, straining his eyes for signs of pursuit, but he saw nothing. He glanced around, noticing a bosque of cottonwoods on the left. He knew that if they took Jason with them, he would slow them down. If the boy was truly dying, then maybe what he was suggesting would be for the best. Old John exchanged a look with the despairing Almira, then he lowered his bulk from the wagon seat, lumbered stiffly to the rear and caught hold of his son's feet. With unusual gentleness, he pulled him from the wagon. He gathered him in his great arms, and Almira and Katie followed him as he stepped towards the cottonwoods. When they rested Jason down, they listened for his breathing, but heard nothing.

'He has gone to his maker,' Almira whispered. 'The Lord giveth, the Lord taketh away. He was a good, God-fearing son. None better.'

'A sweet boy.' Old John nodded and pulled some leaves over the body, building a little mound, but he left his son's head poking out, just in case he decided to breathe some more.

Almira said a short prayer, then reluctantly they turned back to the wagon.

An hour later, they reached the cave and commenced working towards the final fruition of all their labour over the past year.

From the cave, Katie and her mother unrolled the great volume of silk. This had been fashioned into a massive balloon-shaped bag, and coated with gum and milkweed sap to make it airtight. Its size took Katie's breath away. It was bigger even than the inn. The balloon had been encased in a twine net, reinforced with rope, and the base of this was now tied firmly to the sturdy wicker basket they had made. It was some six feet square.

Old John uncapped the gas vent and connected up the earthenware pipe he'd had especially made. This, he ran to the base of the balloon, fastening it by binding around rope. Next he anchored the balloon with rope to four great boulders. With a grunt of pride, he stood back as the balloon inflated, enjoying every moment as he watched his dream coming true. He'd been sacked from his job at the balloon factory in Germany for inefficiency. He wished his old bosses could see him now, see what he had achieved, and admit that he was truly a master craftsman.

Gradually, the balloon inflated with lighter-than-air gas, straining upwards, held by its moorings. They had filled Katie's sacks with sand and fastened them around the basket to act as ballast. When the balloon was fully inflated, it reared above them, blocking out the sky. Old John made a sort of vacuum tube at the base, tying a doubly strong knot with the thickest twine.

He checked the wind, noting that it was blowing towards the south. That would suit him fine, for it would carry them far across Texas — and with night coming on, they would travel unnoticed and eventually descend when they were far enough away to be completely safe.

At last, all was ready. Old John motioned the women to climb into the basket, but Katie held back.

'We must take him.' She pointed towards the unconscious Conroy, who was still in the wagon.

'*Nein*!' her father snapped stubbornly.

'But, Pappi, remember he has got money hidden on him somewhere. We must take him with us. No need to delay here.'

Her father hesitated, then he glanced into the distance. Was it his eyes playing tricks, or did he see riders back there?

'All right,' he grunted. 'We can throw him out when we've found the cash.' Without further ado, he roughly dragged Conroy from the wagon and tossed him into the wicker basket.

Soon, the rest of them had clambered

aboard. Conroy was sprawled like a crumpled doll on the floor of the basket. The others stood over him, the women clinging to each other. There was no space for them to sit down. The old man had carefully loaded the heavy satchel containing the wealth they had accumulated. Soon they would truly be able to enjoy the fruits of their labour. He drew out his knife and leaned over the side of the basket. With a proud flourish he slashed the anchoring ropes, and the basket rose from the ground with a smooth and majestic surge. A moment later and they were lifting into the darkening sky, the greedy wind glad to seize hold of them.

Old John unleashed a triumphant laugh. He was not a sentimental man. He had already forgotten that he had lost his son that day, his mind now filled with pride in his craftsmanship, and satisfaction that he had eluded the vigilantes.

But he would not have been so happy if he had known what the elements held in store for them.

12

The weather was unseasonably stormy. Should the winds become too strong, the balloon might be drawn in a direction that was not ideal. And lightning, too, could prove a hazard. When Old John eventually foresaw the problem, he tried to push it to the back of his mind. It would have to be faced when it occurred.

His reasons for bringing along the senseless Conroy McClure had not been motivated only by his daughter's inane desire to keep the man alive. He'd decided that, for two reasons, it might be unwise to dump the body. Firstly, if found, it would provide any trackers with a clue; and secondly, he was conscious that, once aloft, they might be short of ballast. He would hold on to the weight until it suited him to dispose of it.

He chuckled to himself as he imagined the vigilantes picking over what was left at the cabin, like a flock of buzzards. There'd be plenty to shock them there. But he had the last laugh, because he had the satchel containing the small fortune that the family had worked so hard to accrue. It had been a risky business running the inn the way they had, and holding off suspicion for so long. He figured the family deserved all they had got. And now, with Jason gone, there would be a bigger share for the rest of them.

Wedged against her mother, Katie was feeling surprisingly pleased with herself. She had whispered mumbo-jumbo beneath her breath, secret incantations, calling upon her magic powers to help them get away. And as she did so, she glanced down at the prostrate Conroy McClure, wedged against their legs. She was glad he was still breathing. It was almost as if he was a blissfully sleeping baby, the like of which they'd had at the baby-farm after drugs or liquor were administered.

She could see the horrific wound that Pappi's hammer had inflicted in the side of his skull. Again she told herself that she should never have allowed it to happen, though if she had prevented the blow, heaven only knows how events would have developed. Maybe fate had decreed it this way. If she closed her eyes, the memory of the passion she'd shared with Conroy warmed her mind. The mere thought of it made her groan with ecstasy. She decided that she would do her utmost to save him from expiring. She felt immensely protective. She was weary, and so decided to attempt to sleep, even though she was standing up. If horses could do it, so could she. She did in fact doze off, but was awakened by the bucking of the basket and the roar of the wind tearing at the ropes of the balloon.

That was when she heard her father expressing his intentions to Almira. He was not getting the altitude he wanted.

He figured it was time to jettison some of his ballast. And it wouldn't be the sandbags. They would need those later.

Katie screamed, 'No, Pappi. You can't throw him out!'

The old man unleashed a stubborn roar. 'He is as good as dead. We cannot get any higher without throwing something out. We need height to get over the hills. I tell you, he is going to die anyway.'

The old man was grunting like a grizzly bear as he struggled within the confined space of the basket, his eyes wide in his madness. Roughly, he pushed the women's legs away from the unconscious man.

'Pappi, you *cannot* throw him out!' And then, with desperate inspiration, she added, 'He's probably got the money hidden in his boots. Remember? That's why you brought him.'

Old John thought for a moment, then he nodded and stooped down. His great hands tugged at Conroy's left boot, and with a heave he dragged it off. He would have pulled the leg off as well, had not the boot come free. He plunged his hand into the warm space left by Conroy's leg, and felt about, but his anguished curse indicated that he had not found what he sought. He turned his efforts to the boot's large heel. He ripped it away from the boot, breaking it apart like a piece of cheese. Again he roared with the frustration of finding nothing.

'Maybe the money is hidden in the other one!' Katie yelled across at him.

Her father steadied himself against the swing of the basket, then, with brutal force, he hauled off the second boot, repeating the frantic search, but with the same negative result. There was no cash hidden in those boots, and there never had been.

The frustration was more than Old John Bender could take. He felt he had been tricked, and he needed to vent his fury on a victim. He grabbed Conroy roughly beneath the armpits, was about to hoist him overboard, when the basket touched something solid, sending them all staggering against each other. In the cloud, they'd been lower even than Old John suspected. The basket had bumped against a hillside.

Katie was the first to react. Grabbing up a knife, she slashed at the ropes supporting the sandbags suspended from the sides of the basket. By the time she'd disposed of the third one, the balloon was rising again, lifting into the heavens.

Old John had been so taken aback by the unexpected collision with the hillside, and so admiring of his daughter's prompt action, that his mind slipped from his interrupted activity and he forgot Conroy.

★ ★ ★

It was many hours later. The night was black, except when illuminated by the awesome flash of lightning. Through the dragging hours, they had been buffeted by wind and rain, and were soaked and utterly frozen. Both women had been vomiting and were now totally exhausted from the eternity they had spent standing up. Old John had shown no compassion. He had given the balloon free rein, having little idea where they were going. He consoled himself with the knowledge that a vast distance must now separate them from any enemies.

Every crack of thunder created the impression of being in the centre of a cruel explosion, like the Chinese firework display that had terrified Katie as a child. Now, both women were screaming. Each clap was followed by a flash of lightning, and they seemed enveloped with electric flame. Old John shouted and struggled with his ropes, almost getting thrown overboard himself by the wild swing of the basket. His worst fears had materialized. The whole world had erupted into a nightmare. Here, high in the heavens, they were caught in the blind fury of a hurricane. One touch from the lightning would have the balloon ablaze and plummeting downwards.

But, strangely, it wasn't the elements that brought their downfall.

It was Old John himself.

With their altitude far greater than he would have wished, he decided he must adjust the cord-tied vacuum tube at the base of the balloon.

He balanced his bear-like bulk precariously on the rim of the basket, using the supporting cords to hang on to. Katie watched, petrified. Almira had her eyes tightly shut, her hands clasped and her lips moving as she pleaded to the Lord for salvation. If Old John lost his footing and plunged earthwards, they would stand no chance of controlling the craft themselves. They would rise and rise into the lost eternity of outer space, swallowed in the immensity of the universe.

Old John wrestled with the cords of the vacuum tube, his eyes bulging, his face shining with sweat. He had concluded that the best he could do was to release some gas, deflate the balloon slightly, and allow them to lose height and maybe land. He had no idea what territory lay below, but it was a chance they would have to take.

However, he was having unexpected trouble with the vacuum tube knot. His thick fingers could make no impression. He had fastened it too tightly, and to make matters worse the rain-soaked cord had shrunk. He broke his thumbnail, trying to loosen the knot. It remained as firm as ever. He yelled at Almira to hand him a knife, and she paused in her prayers and struggled to comply, gazing up at him with eyes wide with fear and a face akin to a saucer full of alabaster.

As he struggled, he noted that the wind had turned, spinning them round like flotsam in a whirlpool. He tried to nick the cord with the point of the knife, but with no success. It was drum-tight. Still balancing danger-ously, he decided to make a hole in the balloon above the vacuum tube, and he instructed Almira to pass him up some more cord so that he could tie a further knot above.

Almira lifted a ball of cord to him. He happened to glance down, and through a gap in the clouds, he saw something that made him groan. In the flash of lightning, he glimpsed what appeared to be the writhing of millions of maggots. He blinked hard, straining his eyes, wondering if his senses were playing tricks, then he realized that what he saw were the waves stirring the sea far beneath them, whipped into white horses by the fury of the storm. They had come much further south than he'd imagined, must now be over the Gulf of Mexico.

Even so, he knew he could not risk going any higher, and so he made an incision in the balloon, stabbing the knife-point in above the knotted vacuum tube. But at that very moment, the balloon was caught in a sudden gust of wind, and he was thrown off balance. This proved disastrous, for as he fell, the knife slashed downwards, ripping the small incision into a great gash. The balloon gradually started to deflate. As he lost his grip on the supporting cords, Almira grabbed hold of his legs, dragging him into the basket.

Glancing up, they cried out with alarm. Old John had not imagined his carefully stitched, gum-reinforced balloon would split so easily. Now it was deflating rapidly. Their ascent was reversed; the basket was losing its stability, threatening to tip them out. Within seconds they were plummeting downwards, faster and faster, drawn by their own weight, helpless to do anything but surrender to their fate.

13

It took Jason Bender a couple of days to realize that he wasn't going to die from the gunshot he'd taken. He reckoned he had been hit by a copper-jacket bullet that had passed straight through him. He lay in the thicket where his family had abandoned him, fanning flies away from the hole in his right shoulder. It had turned a swollen blue. He cursed his luck. Had his family been half decent, they would have stayed with him until he'd either packed his bags completely or recovered sufficiently to continue the journey. They should have realized he would change his mind about being left, and perhaps hidden out from the vigilantes until he felt better.

If they eventually reached San Francisco and started enjoying the cash they'd accumulated, by setting up home in a fine house, as their plan had always been, he'd track them down one of these days and remind them that they shouldn't have left him to die alone in the wilderness. His mind seemed to have completely forgotten that he'd pleaded with them to let him rest, that he'd done enough travelling for the time being.

Mind you, apart from being alive, his condition was nothing to write home about. His shoulder wound was still downright misery, and his breathing felt restricted, and if he didn't get something to eat mighty soon, he would die of starvation.

He lapsed into sleep again, and when he woke up later, he realized that flies were clouding around him. But it was not these that had disturbed him; it was voices.

His thoughts swung to Colonel York and his vigilantes. If they stumbled upon him, they'd string him up before he could bat an eyelid.

He grew tense as he heard the rustle

of foliage and the whickering of horses. His right arm was stiff and too painful to move, but he reached around with his left hand and slid his gun from its holster, prepared to make a last-ditch stand. But when the bushes parted, he saw an Indian. A scraggy, old Osage in tattered feathers who must have avoided the Army's sweep, three years back, to round up all wayward Indians and herd them off to agency or reservation.

The old Indian was thin, and had a long nose and receding chin. His small eyes glinted beadily, without expression. Shortly, he was joined by his wife and two young children, presumably their grandchildren. They all looked of poor stock. They stood gazing at the bedraggled white man, surprise registering in their dusky faces.

The old Indian stepped forward, stooped down and peered at Bender, paying particular attention to his wound. After a moment he stood up and muttered something to his wife, who hurried off with the children. The Indian asked Bender a question, but as it was in an Indian tongue he was wasting his breath, and so wandered off, muttering to himself and leaving Bender unenlightened as to his potential fate. Presently, all the Indians returned, bringing with them a v-shaped contraption of poles and blankets, with a platform of animal fibres to support a burden — a travois, with the narrow end hitched over a horse's shoulders. Bender concluded that they were going to drag him along.

At least, he thought, *they are not going to kill me straight away. Maybe they think I might be worth some money to them if they keep me alive.*

Within five minutes, they had lifted him, surprisingly gently, on to the travois and dragged him to where several other horses were tethered. Soon they were on the move.

They travelled for the next hour across rugged terrain, which caused Bender considerable discomfort, but he survived and by nightfall they'd reached a small Indian encampment — four cone-shaped lodges, frameworks of poles covered with animal skins. Soon he'd been fed — a stringy meat stew similar to that which his mother had served to guests at the inn. After he'd eaten, he was bedded down in a tipi. There were three or four families of Osages, along with a half-dozen mangy dogs, all pretty poor, but the Indians seemed willing to share what they had with him, and he did not argue. Certainly, they showed him no hostility.

Next morning had him feeling somewhat stronger, and he was glad enough to allow himself to be pampered by his new-found companions. They even applied some so called medication to his wound. Mind you, the old woman scared the daylights out of him in the process, because he thought she was trying to burn him alive. She cauterized the wound by placing a stem of yarrow into it and setting it on fire. Then she applied the scrapings from animal hide, binding it all over with a poultice of spider webs. Amazingly, he felt better with each passing day. It was lucky for him that the bullet had passed clean through.

There were a couple of young girls, maybe aged seventeen or so, who smiled and giggled at him from behind their hands. Soon after his arrival, they took to wearing long strings of shells hanging from their earlobes down to their waists, all to impress him, but it made no difference to his feelings. He decided that he had never seen uglier females in his life. They looked like wooden blocks with gnarled bits sticking out here and there, and their faces were snub-nosed and evil. If they'd visited the inn, his father would have kicked them out. One of them even made him a pair of moccasins, which he promptly slung to the side and forgot. Had he felt fitter, he would have cuffed the girls away, regardless of the offence it caused, but right now he did not have sufficient strength. But they weren't put off by his inner thoughts, his feigned indifference, and were soon waiting on him hand and foot, sometimes rubbing their overripe titties against him. And all the time their grandfather, who seemed to have replaced their true father, nodded his agreement and smiled to himself.

Bender wondered what their motive was. Why should they care about his welfare? Could it be that they knew who he was? That they were biding their time, trying to keep him unsuspecting, until he could be handed over to the authorities and a reward claimed? But he dismissed the idea that they had tumbled to his identity, for generally redskins weren't interested in such matters as the white man's criminality, glad enough to stay out of trouble themselves. He also considered it an advantage that none of them spoke American, and thus they were unable to pester him with questions that might have been difficult to answer. In fact, he heard only two familiar words, and those were when the old man pointed to himself and said, 'Red Weasel.'

Gradually, a possibility dawned on Bender. Maybe the old man was anxious to be rid of his grandparental responsibilities. Maybe he saw the white man as a suitable husband — twice over? Such matters were not unknown. Bender groaned at the thought. He wanted nothing that would shackle him — but, on reflection, if he did cause insult to these redskins, there was no telling what form their anger might take.

As the days passed, his wound healed, despite its gnawing pain. He played stupid dice games with his hosts. The dice was made of walnut and was tossed in a tea-plate-sized basket, while a woman kept the score on an old abacus. On other occasions they played with sticks marked to represent totem animals. But Bender showed little enthusiasm, because more important thoughts plagued him.

He asked himself over and over what

had happened to the rest of his family. With luck, they would make it to San Francisco and start living it up, the way they'd always planned. He figured Katie could charm any male into giving her what she wanted, and the old man and woman had always taken full advantage of that. Thoughts of Katie made him feel restless. He had always resented the way she spread her legs for strangers. Now his yearning for her was like a fire burning inside him. He was missing her more than anything else in the whole world.

He figured that as soon as he was fit enough, he'd leave these stupid Indians, carefully make his way westwards to San Francisco, and somehow link up with his kin. Though he'd have to make sure they'd gone there before he set out, because it was a mighty long way. He smiled as he imagined the expressions on their faces when he turned up. Maybe Katie would be pleased to see him, welcoming him with open arms — and legs.

He would have resigned himself to allowing matters to proceed quietly until his wound had healed over completely, but one day, about three weeks into his stay with the Osages, a couple of white men rode into the encampment. Bender lay hidden in a tipi, spying out through a split in the entrance flap, feeling downright vulnerable and not liking what he saw. The visitors were clearly bounty-hunters, and were sagging with the weight of their weapons and bandoliers. They talked to the Indians, using their hands in the sign language. They constantly held up a poster which made Bender cringe and want to crawl away and bury himself in a hole. He reckoned, sure as Texas, that the poster was a Wanted notice, and it didn't take much imagination to figure that the name of 'Bender' was displayed prominently on it, and also details of a substantial reward, no doubt.

If Red Weasel understood the implication of what he was being told, he didn't let on. He just kept shaking his head, and presently the visitors seemed to lose patience, returned to their horses and rode away. Bender breathed a sigh of relief.

But the incident had given him a nasty jolt. It wasn't healthy to remain with the Indians any longer, both because of the increasing unrequited intimacy that the young females were inflicting upon him, and, even worse, the likelihood of the bounty-hunters returning.

14

That night, when the encampment had quieted, apart from snoring, Bender took his leave, taking care not to disturb the dogs. He did not pause to express any appreciation to the Indians, not really knowing why they befriended him, nor caring, so long as they never pestered him again.

He hurried through dark forests, putting as many miles as he could between himself and any signs of civilization before dawn poked up.

Two days later, he ambushed an unwary traveller from behind, using an oak-branch club to strike the man's head, smashing it into a bloody pulp. Afterwards, he smiled to himself, because it brought back happy memories of previous hammer-work. He relieved the body of everything of value, including twenty dollars, a Navy Colt, an ammunition belt, clothing and the man's sorrel horse. Thereafter, he set out with renewed determination to track down his folks and enjoy his share of the stolen fortune.

At night, his dreams centred on Katie, made him pant with excitement, had spittle moistening his tobacco-stained lips. He would awake in a swelter of sweat. He was obsessed with thoughts of her body, of her pale flesh, her smooth breasts, the dark, secret places. No other woman could ever satisfy him the way she did. He had to find her, one way or another.

The thought that she might not be alive never entered his head.

Whether or not she was truly his sister did not concern him overly, nor the notion that his lusts for her might be plain unhealthy. Both he and Katie were so unlike their parents, that it was not beyond the realms of possibility that, when the Benders had fancied having a family of their own, they had simply helped themselves to a couple of likely candidates from a baby-farm, not knowing or caring whether they were kin to each other.

But over the next months, any evidence of the whereabouts of his family eluded him. In one newspaper, he read an article about the Bender family and the awful sins they had committed, and he grinned with pride when it described the skilful way in which the family had completely disappeared, leaving vigilantes, lawmen and bounty-hunters all at a loss as to where they had gone. He had to give his old man credit; he had made a good job of preparing the way for escape.

Bender was a loner. He lived like a wolf in the wilderness, gradually recovering from his bullet-wound, though he was concerned that his right arm and his gun hand were not as steady as previously, but he hoped time would restore his strength. He drifted into towns only when he felt in need of a bawdy-house. He stole what he required from the unwary, committing murder several times. He was confident he could avoid apprehension for as long as he had to. But he was not a happy man. He yearned for the money that was due him and, even more so, he yearned for Katie.

In those days, a lot of news took a lengthy time to circulate through the country, the telegraph being already over-subscribed. Newspapers made it a practice to exchange copies, and thus pick up items of interest from far and wide.

It was a good year after the Benders' departure from their notorious inn, when Jason Bender acquired a copy of a newspaper which was running the same story that Conroy McClure had read some months before. Bender's reading ability in English was limited; even so, his heart began to beat as he absorbed the meaning.

Mexican Captain Don Pieppo has arrived in Galveston and related how, in the terrible storms of 1873, his ship ran into trouble in the Gulf of

Mexico, off the coast near the town of Valparado.

Members of his crew were furiously bailing at the pumps when, at about ten o'clock, they heard voices in the dark sky above the ship. A huge deflated balloon dangled in the rigging and collapsed one of the masts, bringing on to the deck a large basket. There were passengers in the basket, but they fell into the sea and were drowned.

Two bodies were subsequently recovered from the sea, those of an elderly man and woman.

'One of my crew,' Captain Pieppo explained, 'identified these as John Bender and his wife, whom he had encountered in Kansas. He had narrowly avoided falling foul of their attempt to rob him. I have since discovered that they were wanted by the law, on charges of murder. Their bodies were claimed by the sea when the ship sank. Fortunately, myself and crew escaped in a longboat.'

Bender had no doubt that the story was true, and the loss of his parents grieved him — and, more so, did thoughts of the fate that had befallen Katie. The newspaper article made no mention of her. Perhaps she had survived. Katie was clever and a survivor, and maybe she had somehow retained the satchel of loot they'd had with them. Bender licked his lips. It was a pretty slim hope — but it was something he had to investigate. The article had mentioned the town of Valparado, down on the Gulf coast. That was where he must now go.

15

'I have some news,' Maria whispered, as they snuggled together in their bed. 'I'm expecting a baby . . . your baby!'

Conroy gasped with surprise.

'How can you be sure?' he asked.

'The same way as every other woman is sure.'

He was breathing in and out fast. After a moment, she wondered if he had misunderstood her. But suddenly he unleashed a whoop of delight.

'Maria, that's wonderful!'

She looked at his face. It was flushed with joy.

'We must make sure our baby grows up into a safe world,' he said.

'We must make sure he gets born, first,' Maria laughed.

'I'll get some wood,' he said. 'I'll make a cot, and maybe a little chair.'

'Or a dolly,' she murmured.

'If he's a girl,' he said, and they both laughed.

He smoothed her hair, gently kissed her forehead and face. They were immensely happy, and this carried over into the days that followed. It was as if they were in a landslide of joy. But the nights were not so happy; his bad dreams did not go away.

Why, he thought, when this new happiness comes to Maria and me, should I still be pestered by nightmares? Again and again, they came to haunt his sleep. The vision of being high in the sky, of swaying back and forth; of clouds and wind swirling around; of hearing shouting in guttural words he could not understand, but knew were expressing terror. He heard the shrieks of the wind, and then felt the sensation of descending at great speed, of having somehow been thrown from a sort of cocoon, to be plunging, plunging. And afterwards . . .

Nothing.

He would awake, struggling, threshing about in the bed — and Maria would be imploring him to understand that he was safe, that there was no danger, that only happiness awaited them.

And frequently he would read the old clipping from the *Galveston Gazette* newspaper, going over it again and again.

He felt certain that the strange incident was in some way related to himself. Maria had explained how she had found him washed up on the shore. Could he really have been one of the ship's crew? But then another possibility occurred to him. The idea of a balloon crashing into a ship sounded preposterous, but was it possible that he had fallen from the balloon? Did he, in fact, belong to this grim family of murderers? He groaned at the idea, plunged his head into his hands, trying to force his brain to remember.

He was trembling at the thoughts that roared through his head. Was he guilty of terrible crimes? Had these hands he trusted, his own hands, which now served groceries to peaceful townsfolk, once had the blood of innocent travellers staining them?

★ ★ ★

Maria had not been feeling well one day, and so she stayed at home. Meanwhile, Conroy served goods and tried to act as if everything was in order, striving to hide his inner turmoil, but in reality he was wondering if the law was already on his trail, and if there were men who hankered to see him dangling at the end of a rope!

When he reached home just after noon, Maria greeted him with her usual cheerfulness, serving a meal of tortillas and eggs, but soon she realized that something was troubling him.

'Tell me. Something is wrong?'

He drew the newspaper article from his pocket and spread it before her. She had seen it before.

'Why are you so worried?' she asked. 'You must've been one of the crew.'

'Maybe I was,' he sighed. 'Or maybe I was not.'

'Does it really matter now?' she asked, an intensity coming to her face. 'We are happy. The past has not been kind to us, neither to you nor me, but we can put it behind us and concentrate on our family.'

'But can't you understand?' he cried impatiently. 'I do not know who I am! I might even be Old Man Bender's son!'

She laughed at him, but it was not a mirthful laugh. 'You are *not* Old Man Bender's son,' she scoffed.

He was taken aback. He had not before seen this scornful side to her nature.

'How do you know?' he shouted. 'How can you be so sure that you are not living with a killer?'

She took a deep breath, visibly calmed herself.

'I *know*,' she said, in a strangely assured voice.

'How!'

'I know because I know *you*!' she replied.

Exasperation caused him to snap inside. He had no answer to give her. How could she be so certain?

Next day, as he worked at the store, he felt he was in some sort of limbo. How much longer could he exist without proving his own identity? How long would it be before investigators appeared, anxious to question him? The problem was that he had no answers to prove his innocence . . . or confirm his guilt.

And then a strange thing happened. That afternoon, in the store, Maria was opening a crate containing melons. She worked on the nails with a hammer, and then stood up straight, to rest her back. For a moment she stood still, looking at him, the hammer in her hand, and the vision of her triggered off a strange sensation in his mind . . . The girl with the hammer. It was as if the scene was repeating something that had lodged in his brain, something from the past. Suddenly, he recalled the words that the local doctor had used when he had examined the wound in Conroy's head: 'It's as if somebody has hit you with a hammer.'

Supposing, he thought, supposing I *was* a member of the crew of that ship; supposing *Maria* was one of the Benders, and *she* had been washed ashore at the same time as I was?

And then perhaps the most alarming question of them all. Could it have been Maria who inflicted this grievous wound on my head?

Conroy swallowed hard, telling himself that it was sinful to allow such thoughts into his head, but instinct warned him that he must watch Maria, that at any time she might revert to her true character. Was she playing some sort of game with him? Was she using him as a shield, to protect her real identity from those who hungered to gain vengeance against the Bender family?

He viewed his wife in a different light, at times cursing himself for being so suspicious of a woman who had acted like an angel towards him — and yet at other times, as strange feelings lurked inside him like shadowy monsters in the depths of the sea, never coming to the surface to show themselves, he discovered aspects of her character that had not been obvious to him before.

Sometimes, when she was unaware that he was observing her, her face would lose its happy expression, and the lines of her features would harden into a seemingly cruel composure. At other times, the scornful aspect of her nature would emerge, and she would show impatience towards him. Friction grew between them, which had never existed before. And yet her kindness towards him did not slacken. She remained considerate and loving, quick to settle any differences they had with her affection and love. He tried to respond, but something had changed within him. A melancholy settled into him, and he debated how long it would be before he actively started to seek his past. So far, love and compassion for Maria had blinded him to the need to discover what had made him what he was. Now he believed he was reaching a stage when such considerations could no longer be pushed aside.

But, he told himself, he could do nothing until the baby was born. He owed Maria the support she needed to see her through her pregnancy and delivery. Afterwards, he must somehow establish the truth, no longer blunder blindly through a life within a vacuum.

Gradually, more recollections were trickling into his mind. He recalled staying at the inn, sitting with his back against a curtain, and people moving about him, talking in their strange German voices. Now, he strained his every sense to visualize their faces. And, after a while, the girl's face solidified in his mind. It was soft, rounded, often smiling . . . *It was Maria's.*

Even her Teutonic voice was the same.

Prof. Miss Katie Bender can heal all sorts of diseases. The words kept running through his head like the catchphrase in some nonsensical song. He reached up, fingered the deep scar that still deformed his skull.

Could it have been Katie who had hammered his skull, intending to kill him, but later had changed her mind for some devious reason, and eventually used her medical powers to restore him to a limited degree of normality? If so, why?

So many questions pounded at him . . . and he was able to find the answers to none of them.

★   ★   ★

Maria boiled some water in a pan and dropped her wedding ring into it, letting it brew.

'Wedding-ring tea can help with the labour pains,' she said, and presently, when the brew had cooled, she poured it into a cup and sipped it down.

Conroy nodded. 'I'll fetch the doctor.'

'No, not yet. Wait until the waters break.'

He didn't argue, but he made her lie down on the bed.

An hour later she complained that her innards felt squeezed, and soon her waters broke, wetting the bed. After a few minutes the labour pains commenced, and they continued for an hour, coming closer and closer together.

He rushed down the street and fetched Doctor Miller, and by the time they returned, Maria was wringing wet with sweat. The pains had become fierce contractions, sweeping over her in a relentless tide, but she was bearing them with great calmness.

'This is not your first time,' Doctor Miller said. It was a statement not a question.

Maria made no answer.

Half an hour later, the baby poked its head out, Maria pushed, and Doctor Miller gently eased the new life into the world. It was a girl, sound in wind and limb. The doctor tied the umbilical cord with thread, then cut it with scissors.

'See,' he said, 'she's a little beauty!'

He held up the moist red body in front of Maria. Then he cleaned the tiny girl with a towel, and passed her to Conroy.

He cradled the baby gently, feeling ham-fisted and overwhelmed with an immense feeling of pride, of creation, as if it was *he* who had given birth. This tiny new life was greeting the world with innocent rage, arms flailing, tiny starfish hands clenching and unclenching, sturdy little thighs and heels churning.

'Let us call her Lucia,' Maria murmured. 'That was my mother's name.'

Once she had ejected the afterbirth, she laid back, totally exhausted, her eyes shining, her cheeks flushed, her hair damp and tangled.

Conroy placed Lucia gently in her arms.

But suddenly the words of the doctor slipped into his mind: *This is not the first time.*

★ ★ ★

Over the next days, he revelled in the joys of fatherhood. The past was forgotten, and he had never known such happiness. Maria gazed at him fondly, a smile on her lips, showing delight in seeing the bond between father and daughter taking hold. At night, with Lucia in his arms, he would pace the floor, singing lullabies, lulling her until her cries subsided. They decided that one day she would conduct an orchestra, for she moved her little arms with such authority.

16

Jason Bender had journeyed southwards across the prairies and ranchlands of east Texas, his pace quickening as he convinced himself that in Valparado he would discover the true fate of his family, and in particular of his sister, Katie. He had studied a map and drawn up plans.

As always, he stayed clear of settlements and towns as much as possible, seeking solace from liquor and women only rarely. His sorrel grew fat on the rich prairie grasses. He hoped that the immediate hue and cry resulting from his family's activities had diminished, although he knew that any reward offered would still stand, and that bounty-hunters were always on the prowl, anxious to make money out of the misfortunes of others. Similarly, there were hostile Comanches and Kiowa to beware of. So he travelled cautiously, and remained constantly alert.

By now his wound had healed over, though his right shoulder and hand still pained him. He practised drawing his gun, firming up his grip, convincing himself that by the time he needed it, he would be able to use his weapon effectively.

He crossed the new railroad track near Fort Worth, spied out on the expanding town with its massive stock-yards and tempting flesh-pots, but decided to skirt it. A week later, in the late afternoon, he reached the rugged shoreline west of Valparado, making certain that he was not seen by a group of fishermen who were bringing their catch ashore and dragging their boats up from the sea.

Excitement was growing in him, for he sensed somehow a closeness to his kin. He wandered the beach, gazing out to sea, imagining what it had been like on that night of the storm. He came across several pieces of wreckage, of flotsam, but nothing that in any way resembled his father's beloved balloon and basket. He even searched the caves that lined the beach, a dream forming in his mind that he might find the satchel of money washed up and lying unnoticed since the night of the shipwreck. He fell to cursing as his searching proved futile.

He returned to the spot where the fishermen had left their boats. He gathered up a fish that had been dropped. It was a baby blue shark. It still writhed with life, and its eye, partly covered by a shield of flesh, gazed blankly at him. He took delight in killing it slowly, jabbing and chopping with his knife.

That night he hid in a cave, cooked his shark over a small fire and wolfed it down. Later, well fed, he rested — but the excitement in him was too intense to allow him to sleep.

Next day, he followed the direction of the fingerboard and, from the conceal-ment of the grapefruit orchard, he spied out on the town of Valparado through the telescope he had stolen from an unsuspecting naval man near the old San Antonio Mission. Unfortunately, Bender had dropped it, causing the lens to crack, but even so he was immensely pleased with the telescope, and it gave him the opportunity to have a good look at the town for anything that might threaten him, prior to riding in. It all looked pretty sleepy and low-key — the quiet streets and plaza, the hotel and stores, the undertaker's — even the marshal's office, with a chubby-looking lawman leaning back in his rocking chair on the veranda, a fat cigar in his lips, a great sombrero shading his eyes.

When he finally rode into town and hitched his sorrel outside the cantina, he was pretty certain nobody would be thinking of the Bender family. In consequence, he openly entered the drinking-establishment and ordered himself a beer. There were no other customers for him to slip into conversation with. He was anxious to ask questions about Captain

Pieppo's ship; anxious to find out if anybody had recollections of any survivors from the tragedy.

Seeing a possible client, one of the saloon's Mexican whores drifted in his direction and struck up a conversation. She was dusky and pretty, though painfully thin. She was no more than twenty, but clearly well-worn. She said her name was Lola. He did not fancy her, but figured she might prove useful.

Within five minutes a price had been agreed. He paid ten dollars upfront, and soon he was ensconced in a tiny upstairs room, scarcely more than a cubicle. It was equipped with the usual bedstead, covered by a bed-tick stuffed with straw. Alongside was a small dresser with a pitcher and bowl, chair and gaudily decorated chamberpot. Quite effortlessly, she slipped her dress off, and she was naked underneath, apart from the bruises that adorned her thin body.

He planted his seed in the girl without finding the pounding exhilaration he had known in the past. No woman could satisfy him the way Katie used to.

After it was over, he asked her how long she had worked in Valparado.

'Two year,' she told him.

'Then you remember when a ship went down in the bay, a year or so back.'

She shook her dark head. She had no recollection. 'Why do you ask, *señor*?'

'Because my sister was aboard the ship,' he explained. 'She was a good-looking woman, with red hair.'

The whore laughed. 'The only good looking women here are us whores, *señor*.'

'You recall nothing of the shipwreck?' he persisted. 'I will pay you for information.'

'No . . . How much you pay?'

'Ten dollars.'

'I will ask Señor Malvern. He runs the cantina.'

He grunted impatiently, and said he would wait in the room until she returned.

His cold eyes dwelt almost scornfully on her body as she rose and pulled on her dress. He felt nothing for her. She could have been a slab of hog-meat for all he cared.

While she was gone, he dressed. Time ticked away. He began to feel uneasy. Was she up to something? Had they somehow become aware of his identity? He rested his hand on the gun holstered at his hip. He was about to leave the room when he heard the girl's steps on the stairs, and shortly she appeared, her face slightly flushed.

'Señor Malvern says he remembers a man and a woman arriving in Valparado at the time of the shipwreck,' she said. 'Maybe he was a survivor. Señor Malvern does not know where the woman came from.'

Bender's interest had quickened. 'What was the woman like? Does she have red hair?'

The whore shook her head. 'I do not remember. All I know is that she had a baby recently.'

'And the man?'

She laughed. 'He is . . . how you say? Ah, yes. A short arse. He runs the hardware store at the end of the street. You should ask him. He will know all the answers to your questions.'

Bender had grabbed his hat, was moving towards the door, a film of sweat glinting on his brow.

'You said ten dollar, *señor*.'

'Which only goes to show,' he said, 'you just can't trust anybody these days!' and he left her with her eyes smouldering and her lips pouting with indignation.

He took the stairs three at a time, rushed out into the street. Now the indifference he had felt when he was with the girl had been replaced by a pounding in his veins. Some instinct told him that Katie was near, that he was on the brink of finding her and solving the mystery of his family's disappearance.

The hardware store, the girl had told him. The survivor from the shipwreck

164

ran the place. Could he be . . . Conroy McClure? Conroy McClure, whose face had given him such a shock when he had first seen it. It was only after McClure had spoken of his twin brother Jesse, that the truth had dawned on him.

Bender had bushwhacked Jesse McClure in the woods near home months before his brother came searching for him. He had killed him with a shot from behind, robbed him of his pittance of cash, and buried him in loamy soil.

Conroy McClure, the second twin, had turned up, and somehow he had lived through the hammerblow to his skull, and the perils of the ocean. And, it seemed, he had dragged Katie with him.

Jason Bender took no interest in the people he passed on the sidewalk, nor they of him, apart from wondering why this big, hard-eyed stranger brushed past them so rudely and walked with a speed not normally associated with the leisurely pace of life in Valparado, particularly so soon after the siesta.

The hardware store was unmistakable, with its stack of buckets, brushes, brooms and gaudy pictures displayed outside. The door stood open. He paused for a moment, pulling the brim of his hat low over his face, loosening his Navy Colt in its leather. He sensed he was about to kill a man, and the familiar excitement was building in him. He took a deep breath, then stepped into the doorway, his big body blocking out the sunlight, creating a black silhouette.

With no customers in the store, Conroy had been counting his takings, spreading the money out in neat piles on the counter. If things remained quiet, he might close the store and get home to Maria and the babe — but suddenly thoughts of them were interrupted as he glanced up and saw the big intruder in the doorway. A wave of disquiet flushed through him. Instinctively, he slid his hand along the shelf under the counter, felt the reassuring solidity of the pistol he kept ready there.

As the stranger stepped forward, Conroy got his first glimpse of the man's face — and beyond its mean look, he experienced no sense of recognition. But he knew that the stranger had recognized him, for his grunt of satisfaction was unmistakable.

'I have come for my sister,' Jason Bender said.

'I don't know who your sister is,' Conroy retorted. 'And I don't know who *you* are.'

Bender snorted with contempt. 'You know who I am! Now stop playing games. Tell me where Katie is!'

'Katie?' Conroy felt the first inklings of recognition filtering into his brain.

'Katie Bender,' Bender confirmed, no longer seeing any point in hedging around the facts. He was anxious to get on with matters. He was going to kill Conroy, but he had to find out certain details first.

'I heard she just had a kid,' he went

on. 'Figured I ought to tell you something, if you're the father. She has had kids before.' He laughed a callous laugh. 'But the little brats did not live more than a few days, because she used a hammer to smash their soft skulls. She'll do the same with this one, for sure.'

Anger burned in Conroy. 'You're lying!' he cried. 'You've come here to make trouble.'

'I speak the truth. Katie was always fond of using a hammer. Say, mister, that's a real nasty hammer-scar you have got on your head. No wonder you are acting like a fool. Guess you had your brains knocked out. Still, it was your fault, coming to the inn. You knew damned well that people had cottoned on to our little business, that the vigilantes were coming after us. No doubt you came to sniff around Katie, like they all did. But she tricked you. I don't know how you and her got out of that balloon when it came down in the sea, but she was pretty good at weaving magic spells. No doubt you did not care much about my mother and father drowning, but I bet you made sure you salvaged that satchel of cash. But it's all over now, mister, because you're going to get what you deserve!'

Conroy's face was glazed with disbelief.

As the final words slid from Jason Bender's lips, the Navy Colt appeared in his hand. He snapped into line, pulled the trigger.

17

Conroy had tensed himself, was dropping down behind the counter as the bullet clove the space he had vacated and collapsed the stacked aluminium buckets behind him into a rattling heap. He grabbed for his own gun, but as he went down, his head struck the brass-reinforced edge of the counter, and everything went muzzy. He was dimly aware of the drum of boots on the sidewalk, then he lost consciousness.

He had no way of telling how long it was before his senses returned. He felt hands grabbing hold of him, propping him up. He smelt men around him, their sweat and the pungent smell of the tobacco they were chewing.

'Hey, you all right?'

The voice was that of the corpulent marshal of Valparado, Tom Kendall. His roughened palm slapped Conroy's cheek, nudging him further along the road to sensibility. Another man was also stooping over him. Enrique Diaz, one of Kendall's veteran deputies, who seemed constantly in a haze of alcohol. Conroy felt in desperate need of air. He pushed himself into a sitting position, forcing those about him to move back.

'We heard the shot,' Marshal Kendall was explaining, 'and wondered what the hell was going on. We haven't heard gunfire in Valparado for years. Who was that *hombre* doing the shooting?'

A strange sense of being focused came upon Conroy, as if yet another blow to his head had rekindled a glimmering of recollection — and in his mind's eye, he saw again the face of the intruder who had come so close to murdering him.

A third man, local barber Arnie Ruger, skinny as a stovepipe, had now rushed into the store, his voice cutting across the words of the marshal.

'Got clean away,' he shouted. 'Headed

out of town. No catching him!'

Jason Bender. The name hammered at Conroy. And then he recalled what Bender had said, about how he was looking for his sister, Katie.

Katie. *Maria?*

Could it be that they were the same person, that on that awful night of the storm Katie had escaped from the sea in the same way as he had, and then taken advantage of his memory loss to pose as somebody else? The possibility brought a curse to his lips — and, with it, a sense of fear. Bender had talked of Katie's previous babies, of the way she had murdered them.

Conroy's skin had gone clammy.

He staggered to his feet, ignoring the pain in his head. He had no idea how much time had elapsed since he had cracked his head on the counter-edge — but one thing was sure: it would have been long enough for Bender to find the woman he suspected was his sister, indeed to have run off with her if that was what she wanted. Or maybe he had committed an even worse crime?

Conroy searched around, snatched up his pistol and, with trembling hands, checked that it was loaded. There was no time to lose.

'I've got to get to my wife,' he gasped. 'She may be in danger!' There was no time to enlarge upon the facts right now.

Marshal Kendall nodded. 'We'll come, too.'

Conroy ran from the store and along the sidewalk, the sheriff and two other men scrambling in his wake. Conroy's lungs were bursting as he reached the ridge overlooking his adobe house. The only movement about the place was the easy rotation of the windmill at the rear of the property. With gun drawn, Conroy went forward, a cold hand around his heart.

He reached the porch. 'Maria!' he yelled.

He paused for a moment, and the only sound responding to his desperate call was the pounding of blood in his ears, and the heaving breath of the marshal and his deputies.

Conroy ran onwards, mounted the stoop and rushed in through the open doorway, knocking a chair over in his haste.

The place was empty, its silence mocking him like Bender's cruel laughter. A movement caught his eye, but it was merely the lace curtains billowing inwardly from the open window.

'Well, there is nobody here, that's for sure.' Marshal Kendall stated the obvious, in breathless tones. He drew off his great sombrero and wiped his brow with his arm. He was a Northerner, but he liked dressing 'Mexican'.

Wild questions were pounding through Conroy's brain, and tangled emotions. If Jason Bender had run off with Maria, or Katie, as fear drove Conroy to believe, had she gone with him willingly? He shuddered at the prospect. He could not accept it. He had felt he had known Maria, everything about her — yet was it all an act she had put on to disguise her true identity? Jason Bender had seemed so positive, so certain, that the girl Conroy had taken for his wife was his sister — and therefore a notorious murderer. And what of the baby, his sweet little Lucia? Had she suffered the same fate as Katie's other babies — a hammer-blow to the skull?

Possibilities swirled within his head like a whirlpool, bringing a cry of anguish to his lips. Whatever the truth was, he'd know no peace until he had unravelled it. He must track down Jason Bender and pray to God that the man had inflicted no evil.

Deputy Diaz had been looking outside. Now he returned, saying that he'd seen the tracks of wagon wheels in the dust outside the adobe, that they'd headed north.

'We must get horses,' Kendall said, replacing his sombrero and trying to stamp his authority on proceedings.

Conroy nodded.

They rushed from the adobe, hurried to the town's hostelry. Five minutes later, the four men, Conroy included, were mounted and riding along the north trail from Valparado, across mesquite prairies. Already night was beginning to close in, their only clue as to the whereabouts of their prey, the faint tracks left by the wagon.

Conroy was totally depressed by the circumstances. But he was determined to find out the truth, no matter how painful it was. And with it, the facts of his own past.

★ ★ ★

As the sun sank, the western sky turned a vivid red, and soon darkness slipped in, taking hold with incredible swiftness, spreading across the prairie like a muffling blanket. Shy jack rabbits had watched as the riders progressed, but now retreated to their burrows.

Marshal Kendall had long since slowed their pace, knowing that the thud of hoofs on the hard earth of the trail would alert any other travellers abroad on this night. Presently, they all drew rein and grouped around to discuss future action. Conroy sensed the general atmosphere of discouragement among his companions, the feeling that they were on a wasted mission.

'Figure there's no point in going on right now,' Deputy Diaz commented, scratching his acne. 'We don't even know if that wagon turned off at some place.'

'You're right,' Arnie Ruger agreed. 'We should turn back. We're way outside the marshal's jurisdiction by now. I say we go back to Valparado and inform the County Sheriff what's happened.'

Marshal Kendall was undecided, but he could see that galloping through the darkness was hardly likely to produce satisfactory results. But he was not keen on turning back. He knew that there was a substantial reward on offer for the capture of any member of the Bender family — and from what Conroy

McClure had said, there could be two of them in the vicinity.

'We will make camp here for the night,' he said. 'We'll carry on searching come daylight.'

'Well, you can do what you like,' skinny Arnie Ruger retorted. 'I'm going back home.'

Enrique Diaz hesitated, then said he would stay on with the marshal.

Within a couple of minutes, Ruger had turned his horse back along the way they had come, and had disappeared into the darkness.

Conroy glanced around at their diminished group. He felt deeply frustrated. Over and over, he had tried to convince himself that his wife was not Katie Bender, but various incidents rose in his mind, seeming to support the possibility. The darkening of her red hair, the mystery over the story of her abusive father, the way she had handled that hammer, her German accent . . . Conroy gritted his teeth, tried to blank such images from his head.

Maria, his Maria, had shown him nothing but love and kindness. How could she be a callous murderer?

But, as time went by, more and more memories were coming to him. He had vague recollections of visiting The Benders' Inn. He struggled to remember Katie's face — but Maria's face kept swimming into his thoughts. He swallowed hard, trying to replace the image with a different one, but his wife's face always returned.

Now, all he could do was hobble his horse, as Kendall and Diaz had done, bed down on the prairie and wait for dawn to come. But he could not sleep. His companions were snoring loudly, and from somewhere way out, he heard coyotes offering up their staccato cries and long-drawn wails. He shuddered, for the sound seemed eerie and unearthly.

But, above all, he was tortured by thoughts of what was happening to Maria and the baby Lucia. *Perhaps they were already dead!*

18

With the first glimmerings of dawn, Conroy was out of his blanket and on his feet. The others, too, were stirring into life, stretching.

It was as they started a small fire and heated some coffee, that a shot boomed and lead whizzed between them like an angry hornet.

As one, they threw themselves to the ground, desperate to find what little cover there was amid tufts of mesquite. Kendall was cursing over and over, his words stinging the air like acid.

Conroy gingerly lifted his head and peered around. He figured that the shot had come from the ridge to the north. Right now, the shadows of clouds, borne on the dawn breeze, were drifting across it, providing movement, but strain his eyes as he might, he could see no evidence of the rifleman. *Heavy-calibre Sharps*, he thought. *Powerful enough to kill a buffalo*. Fortunately, the shot had not been well-aimed, but there was no assurance that the next one would not be.

Knowing that the Sharps was a single shot weapon and time was needed to reload it, Conroy forced himself up and again strained his eyes for sign of their enemy on the far ridge, but there was nothing. Anyway, there was plenty of cover up there. Maybe the marksman was finding a more suitable position from which to fire his next shot — or maybe he was on the move again, renewing his flight.

In all their minds, there seemed little doubt that Jason Bender had pulled the trigger. Perhaps he had aimed at Conroy. This would be his second attempt at killing him. The third could prove successful. He swallowed the bile that had accumulated in his mouth.

Behind him, Marshal Kendall and Enrique Diaz were rising gingerly to their feet, heads sunken into their shoulders, eyes darting around nervously.

'Maybe Arnie was right,' Enrique Diaz said, his facial muscles twitching. 'Maybe there's no point in us playing sitting ducks out here. I've got a wife and two *bambinos* to support.'

Marshal Kendall sighed, shaking his head uneasily. He turned to Conroy. 'How about you? There is not much point in any of us getting our heads blown off.'

'I'm going to follow on,' Conroy said. 'How can I let Bender get away with my wife and daughter?'

'Even if your wife turns out to be Katie Bender?' Kendall asked.

'I'll find out the truth,' Conroy said.

Kendall wavered with uncertainty, but after a moment he nodded. 'Well, that's your decision. It's your life that's at stake. All we can do is wish you well.'

He swung his gaze around, wondering if another shot would soon be forthcoming. It was not a pleasant feeling. If anybody wanted to shoot a marshal, he was an easy target in his great sombrero. If he dispensed with it, the sun would fry him to a frazzle. For some crazy reason, his skin had always been sensitive.

Diaz, too, was impatient to be away.

'Good luck, Conroy,' Kendall said. 'We'll keep an eye on the store till you get back.'

He raised his hand in a farewell wave, and Conroy stood watching as they mounted up and heeled their animals away. They did not look back. They were most likely ashamed of themselves for acting the way they were, but then Conroy concluded that they were, no doubt, as much concerned for the welfare of their wives and offspring as he was for his.

His mind swung back to his own vulnerability. He was stuck in the open, a sitting target for Bender if he was still lurking with his rifle. He decided he had to gamble that the man had moved on, pushing his wagon, laden with woman and baby, to put distance between him and those who knew his identity.

The urgency of the situation impressed itself upon Conroy McClure.

He went to his horse, a chunky claybank, and mounted up. He swung his gaze around the adjacent terrain. The prairie dipped and rose like an ocean, lifting, snagged with mesquite, towards the far ridge. He nudged his animal into a trot, moving towards the ridge, aware that he might well already be centred in the sights of Bender's gun. He licked his dry lips. He was as exposed as a fly on a drum-top. He rode, ready to plunge from his saddle at the first inkling of danger.

It took him twenty minutes to reach the higher ground. He could see why Bender's shot hadn't been accurate. The range was too great. But certainly Bender had achieved something, for he had scared off the majority of his pursuers. Conroy told himself that he would never turn back. He would stick to Bender's back like a flea until he had hounded the man down and recovered Maria and his babe. Maria . . . Katie. The two names jostled in his head, merging into one and the same. Sadness spread through him. The woman he'd loved and respected, the woman he'd taken as his wife, sired her child. Was she . . . ?

No . . . no!

He kicked his claybank for greater speed, his anger flaring.

He rode up the escarpment, seeing the naked line of the crest above him. It was serrated, like the blade of a saw. He kept his shaggy head ducked low, his pistol drawn, his every sense tense as a coiled spring.

He topped out on the ridge, seeing how the land dipped away beyond — an immensity of rolling grassland, speckled here and there by groves of trees. His eyes ached with straining for sight of the wagon, moving like a beetle across the open stretches, but the only movement came from the swirl of birds and the furtive, darting run of a coyote along a stream-side.

He dismounted, searching warily over the ground. Presently he found what he sought, amazed at his luck. A spent cartridge case, lying in a hollow along the crest, a place that afforded a splendid view of the twisting trail. He searched downslope, but could not discover further evidence of human presence. He had anticipated that he might find the indentations left by the wagon's wheels, but there were none.

He returned to the claybank, mounted up and heeled it forward. He was pitting his battered wits against an enemy who might be close at hand or perhaps already far away. He hadn't the remotest idea where Bender would head for. Maybe he had some remote hideaway, where he could hibernate like a grizzly bear until any pursuit had faded away, but what would he do with his captives in the meantime?

Captives?

The word stuck in his craw. Maybe

Katie had welcomed her brother with joy. Maybe the baby had already been disposed of, its poor little skull split open like the other babes Katie had borne. *God, no!*

Conroy reached a shallow stream, the water rising in little diamonds around the legs of his horse. He dismounted, allowing the claybank to suck up liquid but not to repletion; a bloated animal would be no good. As he paused in midstream and quickly refreshed himself, his stomach rumbled. He had not eaten for hours, but there were more important matters to deal with now.

The heat was a throbbing, almost tangible thing, the sky a searing blue, the breeze long since died to nothing. He climbed into his saddle once more, went onward, and the splashing sounds of his animal and the subsequent thump of its hoofs on the far bank seemed strangely loud and echoic, intrusions into a silent world. Remote movement came from a few turkey buzzards cruising on the high thermals.

It was a world waiting for something bad to happen; Conroy could feel it in every fibre of his body.

It took all his courage to force his mount up the far bank of the stream. He topped out on to prairie that was cloaked with mesquite and mottled with shadowy bosques of cottonwood and willow, some as large as copses.

Five minutes later, the shot came, sharp and deadly, cutting across the silence like a sabre!

The sound reverberated, hanging in the air, suddenly awakening a great cacophony of squawking as crows stirred from their siesta and lifted in a black, alarmed cloud from the trees.

Instinct had Conroy dropping from his saddle to sprawl in the tall grass. Gradually, he realized that the shot had not been aimed at him, but had come from within the adjacent copse. And now a new sound probed at his ears — the tiny cries of a baby, and his heart lurched in his chest.

He pushed himself up, quickly

tethered the claybank. He clawed his gun from his waistband and ripped his way through the tall grass towards the trees, Lucia's screams drawing him like a magnet.

And then, entwined with the screams, he heard a horse whicker and a man's voice cursing. Jason Bender's guttural Teutonic tones were unmistakable.

Conroy drew up, standing amid the trees, steadying himself. Now, more than ever, he must not blunder into disaster. He stepped forward, bracing himself for the scene that awaited him. Reaching the edge of the clearing, his fears were confirmed.

The bulky figure of a man, an old man, was sprawled face down by a small fire, a bullet-hole showing in his back. Nearby lay Lucia, wrapped loosely in a blanket, her arms and legs wriggling, her cries desperate. And beyond, Bender and Maria were struggling, his breath coming hoarsely, hers as a gurgling scream constricted in her throat.

'Well, you're not my sister,' Bender snarled, 'but you'll have to do instead!' He was ripping her dress away, exposing her pale shoulders.

Knowing that they were as yet unaware of his presence, Conroy raised his gun and took careful aim at the back of Bender's head. He could not afford to miss, for fear of hitting Maria, but Bender was a writhing target.

Conroy's finger tightened on the trigger. But the gun misfired, emitting only a metallic click.

Realizing they were not alone, Bender thrust aside Maria and turned on Conroy, his eyes radiating the fury of madness. He towered above Conroy, for a second uncertain whether to spring at the shorter man with his hands, or to go for his own gun. Conroy did not give him a chance to reach a conclusion. He hurled his weapon directly into Bender's contorted face, heard the satisfying clunk of metal into flesh and bone. Bender staggered back, spraying blood about, crying out in shock, his hands clawing at his battered features. He tripped over the prostrate form of the old man, half rolling into the fire, his cries of agony intensifying as he was burned.

Conroy stumbled towards Maria. She was gathering up the baby in her arms, desperate to comfort her and quell her weeping. Conroy embraced them both, thankful that they were momentarily safe.

'What happened, my love?' he gasped. 'What happened?'

Tears were flowing down her cheeks, the ordeal she had suffered reflected in her haggard face and wide eyes.

'My f-father,' she sobbed. 'He came to the house, forced Lucia and me into his wagon. He was so brutal . . . said he would kill Lucia if I did not go with him. He said he was taking me home, that he didn't care that I was married, that I belonged at the ranch, looking after him.'

'My God!' Conroy groaned.

'We camped last night, when it got

dark. This morning . . . This morning we moved on, until we stopped here in this wood. It was then this awful man attacked us, killed my father and said something about me not being his sister, after all.' She wiped tears from her eyes with the back of her trembling hand. 'I couldn't understand what he meant. But he came for me, would have done awful things . . . Thank God you arrived! I'm so grateful.' Her gaze had drifted over his shoulder. She suddenly cried out, 'Oh, no! He's gone!'

Conroy whipped round and grunted with dismay. He'd believed that Bender had been knocked helpless. That was not so. The space where he had fallen now mocked them with its emptiness, splashes of blood the only evidence that he'd been there.

Jason Bender had vanished.

19

Conroy retrieved his gun from the ground, where it had fallen after striking Bender. Maria clutched her now quieted baby, and kept guard with frightened eyes, listening for any sound that might indicate fresh danger. Conroy checked the chamber of his revolver, fingering out the cartridge that had misfired. He spun the cylinder, making certain there would be no repetition of the fault. It had almost cost him his life.

Despite all that had happened, he knew that he no longer had to wonder if Maria, his wife, was Katie Bender. He would feel guilty for ever to have suspected her of such a thing. But now was not the time to rejoice.

Suddenly they both tensed as they heard the thud of receding hoofs, coming from beyond the trees.

'That must be him,' Maria gasped. 'He is riding off, thank God.'

'Unless he's tricking us,' Conroy said. 'Maria, we can't relax, not for a second.'

She nodded.

'You say your father had a wagon?' he asked.

'*Ja*,' she nodded. 'He left it at the edge of the wood. It must still be there.'

'We'll fetch my horse, then ride in the wagon back to town.'

'And my father?' she murmured almost inaudibly, and he met her gaze.

'You want that we should take him with us?'

'*Ja*.'

A minute later, with great caution, he led her through the trees to where his claybank stood tethered. They then led the animal back to where the camp was. The fire had now died to ash. For the first time, Conroy got a look at the body of Maria's bullish father. He shuddered at the thought of the violence this monster had inflicted against his wife and daughter. Maria stood watching him, and now there were no tears in her eyes.

He unfastened the lariat from his saddle and tied it around the corpse. Maria gripped the claybank's bridle, calming the beast with one hand, grasping the baby in her other arm. Somehow, Conroy hauled her father's body across the back of the reluctant animal. He secured it with the rope, then they started through the trees, hoping, praying, that Jason Bender was long gone. They found the springboard wagon where it had been left, the mare grazing unconcernedly nearby.

It took ten minutes for Conroy to hitch the mare into the traces and fasten his own laden claybank to the rear of the wagon. Then he helped Maria, still holding the baby, on to the seat, and climbed up himself. He knew it was approaching torrid noon, and that they would not be able to reach Valparado by nightfall. During the afternoon, the wagon would no doubt be seen if Bender was still loitering around, with his big Sharps rifle — or was he so badly hurt that he needed somewhere to rest, or better still to die?

Conroy doubted fortune would be that kind to them.

It wasn't.

★   ★   ★

They travelled through the searing heat of the afternoon, the wagon jolting over the rugged earth. Maria had recovered well from giving birth, but the ordeal of the past few hours had taken a severe toll on her, as had the frequent demands by her daughter for milk. Even so, she strove to remain alert and keep a watchful eye on the surrounding terrain. The strain was intense, for there was no telling when, or if, Jason Bender would reassert his evil presence. If he had survived the facial blow, it was certain he would be burned up with lust for vengeance, and he was not the sort of man to let such a lust go unsatisfied.

By the time the sun had slipped into its westward drift, bringing welcome coolness to the terrain, they had forded a stream, allowing their horses to sup their fill of water. Both Conroy and Maria were totally weary, so they made camp. Fortunately, there were some provisions, including coffee, in the wagon, and Conroy was glad to placate his rumbling belly.

The evening was deathly quiet, the only sound the buzz of flies around the body of Maria's father, which Conroy unfastened from the claybank and laid down a fair distance from where they chose to rest. He hobbled the horses and left them to graze.

He and Maria sheltered in a small dip in the stream's bank, using their saddle and gear to lean back on. But Conroy knew he could not afford to close his eyes. Jason Bender would have no compunction in creeping up on them, murdering them while they slept.

Maria wanted to take a turn at

keeping watch, but he would not hear of it. If ever a woman needed a man's protection, it was now, and he was determined not to fail her. Before she dozed off, there was something he needed to know, for it had plagued him ever since the time of Lucia's birth.

'Maria,' he murmured, 'the doctor said Lucia was not the first time you'd birthed a babe.'

She gave him a concerned look, and he immediately felt guilty for questioning her.

'You don't have to tell me,' he said.

'It is not right that we should have secrets from each other. Each secret is like a brick in a wall separating us. I didn't tell you, because I thought you would be angry.'

He pursed his lips and shook his head.

She took a deep breath. 'I tried to escape my father before. I ran off with a man I did not love. I just wanted to get away. I got pregnant by him, but the child died at birth. And then my father found me, just like he did this time, and dragged me back.' Her head dipped and she wept.

Conroy took her in his arms. He was not angry. No doubt he himself had committed far worse deeds in the part of his life hidden behind the curtain of lost memory. Not that what she had done had been anything more sinful than that motivated by a frantic desire to escape the abusive monster she had for a father. Whatever had happened in the past, there was nobody in the world he loved more than Maria — and little Lucia.

He rested his wife down, covered her with a horse blanket, kissed her forehead and told her to sleep while he kept guard. She did so with the baby pressed against her breast.

Presently he watched as the stars pricked through the blackness of the night sky. He heard the rush of an owl's wings and the scurrying of mice in the grasses, and later a coyote lifted its yapping cry into the night. Periodically, the baby woke, demanding to be fed, and once satisfied quieted for another spell — but apart from these stirrings, he heard nothing else through the dragging hours of darkness.

Come dawn, he forced his bleary eyes to be particularly alert, for he remembered how Bender had struck at first light on the previous day. But today there came no intrusion, and as the new morning took hold, they resumed their journey.

They arrived in Valparado in the late afternoon, unscathed but bone-achingly weary. Conroy handed the dead weight of the old man to the local undertaker, then he sought out Marshal Kendall, who promised to set a guard on their adobe while they took to their bed. Conroy agreed a generous payment for this protection. Finally, he took the horses to the hostelry.

At dusk, he carried out a cautious and circuitous patrol of the land surrounding his adobe. He wondered how long he would have to live in fear of Jason Bender's return. There was no way that he could believe Bender would let the matter rest, if he still survived, and he doubted that the facial blow had proved fatal. His grim conclusion was that his enemy could take his time with any recovery necessary, and then pick his moment to strike. The thought was daunting. He might even have to contemplate moving elsewhere, for Maria and Lucia's sake. But the idea of fleeing like a fugitive from this awful man who had turned their lives into a nightmare went against his grain.

Reassuringly, two of the sheriff's deputies, Carlos Benitez and Pedro Salinas, turned up at the appointed time for their night duty. Both men were grey-haired. They were armed, and agreed to fire three shots of warning if there was any cause for alarm during the hours of darkness. They did not accept the duty with much grace, but ten dollars per stint was not to be scoffed at. They took up position in the shrubs adjacent to the adobe, and promised to remain alert. Conroy wished them goodnight.

The air was raucous with the sound of cicadas, and the heat was heavy and oppressive. Maria was particularly concerned that Lucia should have enough air, and so they decided to leave the windows open. Conroy was not happy about this, for he felt tempted to barricade the entire place, but obviously the baby's needs were paramount, and he consoled himself with the hope that the guards would remain alert.

Maria fed the baby, and then the couple took to their bed. Conroy was soon satisfied that his wife was sleeping soundly, but he could not sleep. The image of Jason Bender's mutilated face kept intruding into his mind, and an inner instinct warned him that the man was close, prowling through the darkness like a hungry wolf. Presently, other concerns occurred — the constant crying of Lucia, who tonight seemed unsatisfied with her feeding. Both Maria and Conroy paced the floor with the babe in their arms, trying gently to lull her to sleep. Only in the small hours did she grow quiet, and husband and wife found their own peace. But both were awake at first cock-crow.

Thankfully, the night had passed without danger. But for how long could their nerves stand the threat of menace? Conroy reckoned that, sooner or later, he would have to undertake the hazardous task of discovering Bender's fate.

20

It was the fourth night since the guards had been mounted outside Conroy's adobe, and it was a tedious and boring duty, despite the ten-dollar payment. Carlos Benitez had not taken the duty too seriously and had dozed there, crouched in the brush, more than once, lulled by the pulsating racket of the cicadas. He somehow ensured that he was awake by the time his employer checked each morning. He knew that his *compadre*, Pedro Salinas, was positioned, hidden up, behind the adobe, and he was relying on him raising any alarm that was necessary, though he was sure in his own mind that this precaution was a complete waste of time.

But this fourth night, unbeknown to Carlos Benitez, Salinas had felt so sick from overeating at supper-time, that he had gone home to recover, convinced, like Benitez, that whether or not he was crouching in the brush, blessing his night-cloaked surroundings with an occasional glance, made not one iota of difference to the passage of events — or non-events, as he foolishly suspected.

In consequence, Jason Bender approached the adobe, drifting through the shadows unimpeded.

Neither Conroy nor Maria had known real restfulness for nigh a week, what with the mental turmoil caused by their ordeals, and the natural demands of little Lucia to be fed at least thrice nightly. Midnight had slipped by, and now, at last, husband, wife and babe, in a cot adjacent to her parents' bed, had lapsed into slumber. They were not aware of the shadow that eased along their veranda and found access through the open window of the main room.

Five minutes later, the nightmare erupted into reality.

'Wake up, you two! Wake up and keep your mouths shut. Any noise, and the baby is dead!'

Maria could not, in fact, prevent her scream of sheer horror, but she stifled it almost immediately, sitting bolt upright in the bed. Conroy too had been jounced from sleep, fear pumping through every vein, eyes suddenly wide open. The silhouette of a man clearly showed against the moonlit window. He was crouching over the cot, and Conroy knew instantly that it was Bender and that he had his gun pressed against Lucia's tiny head.

His stench of sweat and unwashed body filled the room, but even more menacing was the deadly intent, the unmitigated evil, that he radiated.

For a wild second, Conroy debated thrusting his hand downwards, grabbing his gun that lay on the floor alongside the bed, but concern for Lucia's life restrained him. He could hear Maria panting like an animal caught in a trap.

Jason Bender chose to laugh. He knew he had them completely at his mercy. There was nothing they could do but submit to his demands.

Right now, Lucia, completely ignorant of the fact that her little life was close to termination, unleashed her cries, but Bender's rough hand grasped the child, lifted her almost weightless body from the cot and clutched it against his chest. His other hand gripped his gun.

'Unless you want the brat's brains blown out,' he cried, 'the woman comes with me. Like I've said, she may not be my sister, but she is so damned like her she'll have to do instead!'

The word erupted from Conroy's lips. 'No!'

'Then I press this trigger and blow your little treasure to bits!'

'No, no, no!' Maria screamed, rising from the bed. 'Don't harm her. I'll come.'

She rushed across the floor, stood alongside Bender. He grunted approvingly, and with a sudden movement jerked his arm to throw the baby at

Conroy, who caught her with thankful hands. He hugged her protectively, trying to quell her terrified cries.

Meanwhile, Bender had moved quickly, unfastening a short coiled rope from his belt. One end was fashioned in a noose. He thrust it at Maria and snarled, 'Put it over your head.'

She was swaying as if in a trance, dazed, but he pushed the noose into her hands and she tremblingly drew it around her neck. He was going to lead her like a dog. However, he had one final act to complete. The pain in his face, the nose broken and pushed to one side, the dreadful cut and bruising across his cheekbone — all were caused by Conroy's thrown gun. Bender had sworn that no man would ever treat him this way — and survive.

He turned his gun towards Conroy and pulled the trigger, the weapon's reverberating blast filling the room, its orange flame stabbing death across the silver of moonlight.

The crack of gunfire brought Deputy Carlos Benitez out of his snoring slumber. He dragged the dribble from his lips with the back of his fat hand and cursed. He belched and forced himself to his feet, rearing above the low shrub to peer towards the moonlit adobe. Immediately, the scurry of movement caught his eye and he heard the strangely choked cries of the woman. A tall man, a seeming giant, was dragging her from the house by a rope, jerking at it to hasten her.

He snatched his gun from its holster, steadied himself, took aim at the fleeing couple — and hesitated. He couldn't risk a shot, for fear of hitting the woman. Now, it was too late anyway. They had disappeared into the grapefruit groves, no doubt following the trail to the beach.

Benitez realized that this was what he and Salinas had been hired to prevent, and with a sinking feeling he knew they had failed. But Salinas should have spotted the intruder. Benitez reckoned that it was the fault of the other deputy, that just when he had relied upon him, he had let him down — badly.

He decided to see what had happened to the husband.

Benitez blundered into the adobe and heard cries. He went into the bedroom and saw Conroy sitting slumped on the floor, his head bowed as he cradled the baby in his arms, his anguished sobbing bringing shudders to his body. Even in the moonlit gloom, Benitez could see the darkness of blood staining his nightshirt.

'Good God, man!' Benitez shouted. 'What has happened?'

Conroy did not answer. Cradling the baby with great tenderness, he stepped over to the cot and carefully rested Lucia down where scant minutes earlier she had been sleeping peacefully.

'Get a lantern,' he snapped at Benitez.

The deputy nodded, found a lantern

in the living-room and struck a match. A moment later he had returned to stand alongside Conroy, and they gazed down at the tiny body in the cot. She was quite dead, no doubt the bullet still in her. Blood was everywhere.

Conroy's voice was quavering with anguish. 'See to her.'

He turned, tears blurring his eyes, fury making his breath come in great gasps.

'They headed through the grapefruit grove,' Benitez muttered. 'I guess they were making for the shore.'

Conroy did not even stop to gather up his gun. He just wanted Bender's throat in his hands, to choke the life out of his evil body, to rid the world of the scum that had destroyed his sweet little Lucia. Grief struck him like a hammer-blow, had sobs rising in him. He couldn't believe what had happened.

He ran now, legs driven by blind hatred.

Still in his nightshirt, he raced like a ghostly spirit through the grove, the moonlight blotted out by the leafy fronds. Shrubs tore at his legs, but he had lost feeling. Nothing mattered apart from catching Bender. *Please God, let me get to him before it's too late!*

He had no true idea where Bender would take Maria, what he would do to her, but he knew she would slow his progress. Somehow, the idea of the cove where the fishermen's boats were dragged on to the sand loomed in his mind. Maybe Bender would use the sea as his route of escape.

Soon the roar of waves against the shore came to his ears, and he increased his pace, desperation giving him a second wind. He wished he had brought his gun, but by now it was too late.

Following the path, he was again in moonlight, the sound of the sea growing louder. Presently, he stopped, holding back on his heaving breath to listen — and sure enough he swore he heard Maria's faint cry. It spurred him forward, and as he ran the distance had never seemed greater. But at last he was approaching the cove, his eyes frantically scanning ahead for signs of movement.

He spotted them — dark figures against the light background of foam. The sea was turbulent, the waves taking hold of the skiff that Bender had dragged into the shallows. Maria was already on board, sitting in the stern, bracing herself against the rise and fall of the small craft, her face a pale oval in the moonlight.

Bender pushed off and leapt aboard himself, reaching for the oars. The skiff took to the swells reluctantly, smacking its wooden prow into each wave. Conroy knew that he must act quickly. Having no wish to be impeded by his nightshirt, he drew it off over his head and ran naked down the beach. He was maybe thirty feet behind the boat as he reached the sea, lunging in great strides into deepening water before the slap of waves slowed him. He dove forward, arms and legs pushing him to greater depth. He swam fast, turning his head to the side to draw in breath. Beneath him, the ocean floor dropped precipitously.

At first, he was unsure if he had been seen, but as he glanced ahead he saw that Bender had laid aside his oars and was standing over Maria, the moonlight glinting on his pistol, which he was aiming at Conroy. Conroy ducked as the orange flash of the gun showed. If the bullet went anywhere near him, he was unaware of it.

When his head broke the surface, he was closer than he had expected. As he flicked his hair from his face, he saw Bender looming above him, standing in the boat with his pistol aimed. At this range, he could not miss. But in that fleeting instant, at the side of his vision, he glimpsed Maria rising to her feet. With the rope still around her neck, she was tethered to a cleat. Even so, she somehow reached Bender, rammed her shoulders against the back of his thighs.

He staggered, then toppled overboard in a great splash, the gun flying from his grasp.

Thrusting his legs backwards, Conroy propelled himself at Bender, threshing wildly in the water. Caught unaware, Bender twisted and attempted to haul himself back into the boat, but as he clawed at the side, his weight sagged the craft downwards. Water was sloughing into it, causing a complete capsize, sending water spuming up. Conroy got his hands around his enemy's throat, trying to pull him under the water, and there was a moment of wild confusion. Conroy was aware that Maria had been thrown into the water, and he was terrified that, still tethered by the rope, she might well be dragged under. Now, as Bender clawed himself free, there was no sight of her.

Conroy was immediately caught in a desperate struggle for his life. Although seething with hatred for Bender, the man's immense strength completely outmatched his own. His only defence was his wits.

Bender had shrugged off Conroy's grip from his throat. He was snarling like an animal. Conroy grabbed his enemy's belt, ramming his knee up, trying to find his groin, but the murderer was writhing and twisting in the water, seeking to find a grip himself. His fingers clawed into Conroy's hair and he turned in the water, dragging the smaller man's head beneath the surface. Conroy attempted to dive deeper, to free himself, but Bender was lashing out with his boots and knees, catching him in the ribs.

Bubbles were swirling around Conroy's head as he strove to break the surface. He could not. He was being held under by Bender's cruel strength and could feel his senses going. Water swirled into his lungs, and in sudden panic he knew he was losing this fight, that hatred for this man, and even wits, were not enough to defeat him. And

Maria! What fate could she expect, if she still survived, at Bender's hand?

Conroy's nightmares of the deep were now for real. But stubbornness goaded him. He could not forsake Maria. He was trying to cobble together his waning senses for one final effort, when agony lanced through his left leg. For a second, it seemed, he blacked out.

When his awareness returned, he knew he was free of Bender's vice-like grip. He did not know why or how. His head had broken the surface. Above the roar of the sea, another dreadful sound was erupting. At first, he couldn't understand what it was. Then, realization hit him. It was Bender. He was screaming, hoarsely, insanely — but he suddenly stopped.

Conroy vomited, spewing up a great volume of salty water. Now, as he rose and dipped in the swell, he regained his breath and tried to make sense of the situation. He could not see Bender. Nor could he see Maria.

He sensed that the water about him had changed; it had darkened, thickened. He was swimming in blood. It was his own.

Shark! The thought struck him like a bullet.

He reached down to feel for his left leg, treading water with the other. Frantically, he groped about, fearing that his fingers would touch the nub of bone, tattered flesh, but he encountered only nothingness. He reached into the air, flexed his fingers, cursing their numbness, then he again stretched down. This time he made contact with his flesh, and he reached further to touch his knee, his foot. His leg was still there, though in what state he could not tell.

His relief was short-lived.

The shark broke the surface, no more than twenty feet away. Twice, it rolled, creating a tidal wave in the water, the white of its huge belly showing. Conroy caught a sight of Bender in the water. Then, having righted itself, the fish's great conical head reared up, its jaws snapped around the villain's body. Bender's head jutted from one side, his booted feet from the other. When the shark submerged with its prey, it left a great shower of foam in the air.

Conroy had watched with stunned eyes. It was almost as if the giant fish had put on the show of defiance for his benefit. He stilled himself in the water, scared that at any moment he might feel the agony of shark teeth in his leg, that he would be dragged under to join Jason Bender. But behind him, he could see nothing in the rise and fall of the sea.

What had happened to Maria?

He groaned, swung his gaze towards the shore. A white line of foam showed where waves broke upon the beach.

And then he spotted her, standing on the shore, her white nightgown like a beacon of exultation.

He forced himself through the water, desperately conscious that his blood was spreading about, desperately conscious that it could draw the shark to him for another attack. Unless it was too busy with Bender.

He struggled towards the shore, and at last his feet touched sand. Twice he fell, face down. Twice he struggled to his feet, beating hard with his arms, blinking with the salt stinging his eyes — but at last the surface rose only to his hips and he reached the shallows, feeling the drive of the waves behind him, the powerful suck of the undercurrent striving to prevent him from escaping. But nothing would stop him now. Finding renewed strength, he reached the shore, and the arms of his wife.

There were no words between them as they clung to each other, their bodies communicating the relief they felt, both of them stained with the blood that flowed from the tattered flesh of his leg. Why the creature had turned from him to seize Bender, Conroy would never know.

Jason Bender, who had emerged from the past to terrorize them and many others, was gone. But as Conroy felt the warmth of his wife's embrace, of her love, he knew he must steel himself to tell her of Lucia's death, that the brief light that had shone in their lives was no more, that the babe had saved his life, by taking the bullet that was destined for him.

He knew that their loss would destroy Maria — and just as she had saved him, given him the strength to survive when he had been washed ashore that terrible night of the storm, so he must do the same for her, and they must rebuild their existence, heal their physical and mental wounds, with love and patience.

★ ★ ★

A week later, husband and wife, still numb with shock, walked along the shore. Conroy used a crutch for support, his emaciated, heavily bandaged leg a grim reminder of events. He would carry the scars for life, deep, angry-red, but he considered them a small price to pay for survival.

Maria's face was utterly drawn, her eyes red-rimmed. She had sat for hours, hugging her baby, until the tiny coffin had been prepared.

As they slowly progressed, an object caught their attention, washed up from the sea. It was a man's boot, and as Conroy stooped to inspect it, a tremor went through him. His nostrils widened to the sickly-sweet stench of decomposed flesh. He picked up the boot, peered inside and saw the reddened, splintered bone of a lower leg, torn off mid-shin.

'Is it . . . ?'

'Bender's boot,' he said.

Higher up on the shore, they scooped out a deep hole and buried the boot, shutting it away for evermore. The boot was gone, but the memory of the man who had worn it would always be with them.

It was two years later that husband and wife purchased land to the north, and some longhorns to graze upon it. They built a house and extended it through the subsequent years, and their holding became a ranch that flourished. So did their family, to the extent of three sons and a daughter.

Gradually his recollections of the past returned to him, both in reality and by association. The body of Katie Bender had never been found, so it appeared obvious that she must have drowned at the same time as her parents. Perhaps she, too, had been devoured by the denizens of the deep.

So Conroy no longer felt himself wandering through the mists of his memory. Now he cherished his foothold on the earth, here in south Texas. His love for his wife had grown forever deeper. And his dynasty would spread and grow, becoming a solid extension of his own being.

We do hope that you have enjoyed reading this large print book.

Did you know that all of our titles are available for purchase?

We publish a wide range of high quality large print books including:
Romances, Mysteries, Classics General Fiction Non Fiction and Westerns

Special interest titles available in large print are:
The Little Oxford Dictionary Music Book, Song Book Hymn Book, Service Book

Also available from us courtesy of Oxford University Press:
Young Readers' Dictionary (large print edition) Young Readers' Thesaurus (large print edition)

For further information or a free brochure, please contact us at:
Ulverscroft Large Print Books Ltd., The Green, Bradgate Road, Anstey, Leicester, LE7 7FU, England. Tel: (00 44) **0116 236 4325 Fax:** (00 44) **0116 234 0205**